CONTENTS

Introduction

Stress and Anxiety is the hundredth volume in the **Issues** series. The aim of this series is to offer up-to-date information about important issues in our world.

Stress and Anxiety looks at young people and stress, stress in the workplace and ways to cope with stress.

The information comes from a wide variety of sources and includes:
Government reports and statistics
Newspaper reports and features
Magazine articles and surveys
Website material
Literature from lobby groups
and charitable organisations.

It is hoped that, as you read about the many aspects of the issues explored in this book, you will critically evaluate the information presented. It is important that you decide whether you are being presented with facts or opinions. Does the writer give a biased or an unbiased report? If an opinion is being expressed, do you agree with the writer?

Stress and Anxiety offers a useful starting-point for those who need convenient access to information about the many issues involved. However, it is only a starting-point. At the back of the book is a list of organisations which you may want to contact for further information.

*****

Coping with stress

Information for young people

About this information

This is from one in a series of factsheets for parents, teachers and young people entitled *Mental Health and Growing Up*. The aims of these factsheets are to provide practical, up-to-date information about mental health problems (emotional, behavioural and psychiatric disorders) that can affect children and young people. This article looks at what stress is, what causes it and how it might feel to be suffering from stress. It also gives some practical advice about how to cope with different types of stress.

Introduction

What is stress?
Everyone feels stressed at times. You may feel under pressure, worried, tense, upset, sad, angry – or maybe a mixture of uncomfortable feelings. There are many ordinary situations that can make you feel stressed. For example, your school work may pile up, preparing for exams may seem as if it's taking for ever, you may be being teased or bullied at school, or having problems with teachers. At home you may be arguing with parents, brothers or sisters, or close friends.

Stress can be even worse if your family is breaking up, someone close to you is ill or dies, or if you are being physically or sexually abused.

The effects of stress

Stress can affect you physically. Your body is designed to be able to cope with stresses such as danger, illness and emergencies. This is called your 'fight or flight' instinct, where hormones such as adrenalin and cortisol gear your body up to cope with immediate stressful situations. For example, if you accidentally step into the road when a car is coming, adrenalin will pump around your body enabling you to jump out of the way of the car – this is your 'flight' instinct coming into play in a short-lived stressful situation. Your body is less able to cope with longer-lasting pressure. This can make you feel tired, make you go off your food and find it difficult to sleep. You may get stomach-aches or headaches.

Everyone feels stressed at times. You may feel under pressure, worried, tense, upset, sad, angry – or maybe a mixture of uncomfortable feelings

---

Stress can affect you mentally as well as physically. You may find it hard to keep your mind on your work, to cope with frustration or to control your temper. You might get depressed. Stress that goes on for a long time can be exhausting.

Understanding and support from other people can make it much easier to cope. If you have someone you can trust to talk to, this can help. Feeling alone makes it harder.

Coping with stress

There are several things that you can do to help yourself cope. For things that happen every day, it can be useful to think of your stress as a puzzle to be solved:

- Think about the situations that stress you, and how you behave.
- Think about how you could behave differently in these situations, so that you would feel more in control.
- Imagine how other people might behave if you acted differently.
- List all the things you can think of that would make life easier or less stressful – write them down on a piece of paper. This can help you sort things out in your head.

Where can I get help?

Sometimes stress gets on top of you. Especially when the situation causing the stress goes on and on, and the problems just seem to keep building up. You can feel trapped, as if there is

no way out and no solution to your problems. If you feel like this, it is important to get help. People you might want to talk to:

- parents, a family member or family friend
- a close friend or carer
- a school nurse, teacher or school counsellor
- a social worker or youth counsellor
- a priest, someone from your church or temple
- the Samaritans (telephone 08457 909090).

Your general practitioner or practice nurse may also be able to help. They may suggest that you see someone from your local child and adolescent mental health service – a team of professionals specially trained to work with young people. They include child and adolescent psychiatrists, psychologists, social workers, psychotherapists and specialist nurses. You should get help if . . .

- You feel that stress is affecting your health
- You feel so desperate that you think about stopping school, running away or harming yourself
- You feel low, sad, tearful, or that life is not worth living
- You lose your appetite and find it difficult to sleep
- You have worries, feelings and thoughts that are hard to talk about because you feel people won't understand you or will think you are 'weird'
- Stress is making you hear voices telling you what to do, or making you behave strangely.

It is possible that you are depressed rather than stressed if you feel these things. If so, it is very important that you get specialist help as soon as possible. Your general practitioner will be able to help.

References

Carr, A. (ed.) (2000) *What Works with Children and Adolescents? A Critical Review of Psychological Interventions with Children, Adolescents and their Families.* London: Brunner-Routledge.

Rutter, M. & Taylor, E. (eds) (2002) *Child and Adolescent Psychiatry* (4th edn). London: Blackwell.

Scott, A., Shaw, M. & Joughin, C. (eds) (2001) *Finding the Evidence: A Gateway to the Literature in Child and Adolescent Mental Health* (2nd edn). London: Gaskell.

- The above information is from the Royal College of Psychiatrists's *Mental health and growing up* factsheet 32. For further information visit their website which can be found at www.rcpsych.ac.uk or see their address details on page 41.

Anxiety and stress

Information from Lewisham Child and Adolescent Mental Health Services

By Geraldine Baker

Although many people will experience stress and anxiety to varying degrees, between 5% to 10% of young people will have anxiety problems that are bad enough to affect their ability to live a normal life.[1]

Signs of anxiety and stress can manifest in young people in different ways; some may feel low or sad, may lose their appetite or find it difficult to sleep. Others may become so fearful, tense or panicky, they experience strong *physical* feelings, which give rise to panic attacks. These can cause a young person to shake, sweat or have palpitations that can leave them feeling breathless.

Anxiety and stress can also leave a young person with thoughts that life is not worth living. Others can become so desperate they may think about running away, feel unable to go out or go to school, may consider taking an overdose or harming themselves in some other way.

There are times when young people may have thoughts about real or imagined experiences, often triggered by traumatic events that may leave them with overwhelming feelings of fear, causing anxiety or stress. This can result in them developing phobias, which can sometimes impact on their day-to-day life.

Bullying, bereavement, physical, emotional or sexual abuse, neglect, domestic violence, parental ill health, exams, relationship difficulties with peers and parental separation, can all leave a young person feeling anxious and stressed.

Therapeutic support is recommended when anxiety and stress is affecting a young person's everyday life. It is important they have the opportunity to gain support from someone who will listen to and understand them, and who can also enable them to find alternative ways of coping with their feelings.

Reference

1. Royal College of Psychiatrists *Mental Health and Growing Up* Factsheet [14] 1999, London

- This information is an extract from *A Guide to Adolescent Mental Health*, by Geraldine Baker.

Exam stress

Information from CALM

Whether it's at school, college, university or taking a driving test, at some point we all have to take exams. For some it's no big deal, for a few it's actually fun, but for most of us exams equal stress and sometimes depression.

So what is stress? Stress isn't all bad. It's what gives that rush of adrenalin that raises your game when you're faced with a challenge. But too much stress can cause anxiety and tension.

It can make you tired, angry, frustrated and down.

Calls to the CALM helpline from students suggest that exam problems are their most common cause of anxiety. The emphasis placed on success by the institution, parents and themselves can be overwhelming. It can seem that the opportunities and choices available are determined in a couple of hours, regardless of the work put in over years.

Steps to ease the stress

Many people think exam stress is a teenage problem, but it can happen to people of all ages. If you're a student worried about exam difficulties, or if you're stressed about something else at exam time, there are certain steps that can help ease the effects:

- Manage your study. Break up periods of work with relaxation. You can only absorb information for so long before it becomes confusing.
- Eat properly and avoid junk food and alcohol, but plan a big party for when the exams are finished.
- Sleep – stress can disrupt sleep patterns. Take time to relax before going to bed.

Many people think exam stress is a teenage problem, but it can happen to people of all ages

---

- Keep busy. When you're not studying do things you enjoy.
- Be nice to yourself – you may feel silly but tell yourself you're great and you can do it – positive thinking and visualising success in the exam can help.

- Failure is not the end. If you don't do as well as you'd hoped talk through your options with lecturers or teachers. You can always re-sit.

Get help and advice

It's important to realise that no matter how much the prospect of exam failure is getting on top of you, you can get help – don't sit and worry on your own. No one can sit the exams for you, but you may be able to get some handy hints from your family, friends, student advice centres, or your teachers/lecturers. Or if you just want a conversation with someone completely objective, CALM's non-judgemental advisors speak to loads of students going through the same sorts of things.

- The above information is from www.thecalmzone.net CALM, the Campaign Against Living Miserably, raises awareness of depression amongst young men across Manchester, Merseyside and Bedfordshire. Even if you can't talk to a mate or a relative, you can talk to CALM on 0800 58 58 58 at any time from 5pm to 3am.

© Crown copyright

Major rise in exam stress calls to ChildLine

The number of young people calling ChildLine because they are struggling to cope with the pressure of exams has risen by over 50% – the biggest annual increase since the charity began taking calls – according to figures released by the charity today (27 May 2004).

During the last year (1 April 2003 to 31 March 2004) more than 900 children and young people called ChildLine's free, 24-hour helpline about the stress caused by their exams – up from just over 600 during the previous twelve months. Thousands more requested a copy of ChildLine's *Exam Stress and How To Beat It* leaflet or visited ChildLine's website for help and advice on coping with exams.

ChildLine's Chief Executive, Carole Easton, said: 'Exam stress affects almost every child at some point in their education and we are hearing from hundreds of children at this time of year who are struggling to cope with the pressure they are under. It is vital to reassure children that there is life after exams, that they are not the only route to success, and that they will still be loved and valued no matter how they perform.

'Some children who call ChildLine tell us that exams are the "last straw" in their young lives – they may be suffering abuse, their families may be going through a break-up or they may be being bullied. Tragically a small number of children who call ChildLine have harmed themselves or have even attempted to commit suicide because they are struggling to cope with the pressure of exams.

'ChildLine urges the Government to carefully consider any measures that could reduce the burden of exams on our young people. Everyone who cares for and works with children needs to look out for warning signs that a child may be struggling to cope with exams and be ready to offer them the support they need.'

ChildLine
0800 1111

In addition to its helpline service ChildLine works closely with schools across the UK through its ground-breaking ChildLine In Partnership with Schools (CHIPS) programme. CHIPS workers raise awareness of ChildLine's helpline service and also help schools to develop peer support schemes that enable pupils to look out for each other.

Head of CHIPS Lindsay Gilbert said: 'Young people tell us that they often feel there is no way out of the pressure they are under at exam time. They worry about letting their families down or what will happen if they don't get the results they need.

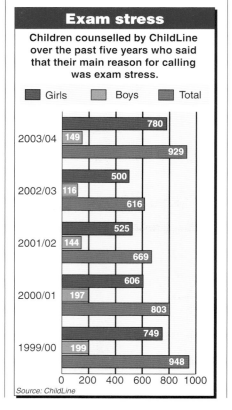

Exam stress

Children counselled by ChildLine over the past five years who said that their main reason for calling was exam stress.

Legend: Girls, Boys, Total

- 2003/04: Girls 149, Total 780, overall 929
- 2002/03: Girls 116, Total 500, overall 616
- 2001/02: Girls 144, Total 525, overall 669
- 2000/01: Girls 197, Total 606, overall 803
- 1999/00: Girls 199, Total 749, overall 948

Scale: 0 200 400 600 800 1000

Source: ChildLine

By training young people as peer supporters we can equip them with the skills and understanding to act as a first port of call for younger children who are struggling to cope with problems like exam stress.'

■ ChildLine's leaflet for children and young people – *Exam Stress and How To Beat It* – is available to download at www.childline.org.uk/pdfs/examstress.pdf or by writing to ChildLine, Freepost NATN1111, London E1 6GL. To find out more about how ChildLine works with schools go to www.childline.org.uk/Schools.asp

ChildLine looked at the number of children calling about exam stress from 1 April 2003 to 31 March 2004 and found that there had been a 51% rise – from 616 to 929 – in the number of children counselled about the issue compared to the previous year's figures.

ChildLine works closely with hundreds of secondary schools as part of its ChildLine in Partnership with Schools (CHIPS) programme. CHIPS is a unique outreach and training programme working in partnership with young people in schools and other settings. In particular the programme encourages schools and youth groups to set up projects tackling issues like bullying and provides support, training, information and resources to help them do so.

ChildLine is the UK's free, 24-hour helpline for children and young people. Trained volunteer counsellors comfort, advise and protect children and young people. The number for children to call is 0800 1111. Lack of funds means that lines can be busy, so children may have to redial several times before they get through.

■ The above information is from ChildLine's website which can be found at www.childline.org.uk

Exam result stress

Exams and the anticipation of results can be a stressful time

What is stress?

Stress is the reaction people have to excessive demands or pressures, such as passing exams. You may find it difficult to cope with tasks, responsibilities or other types of pressures or you might get anxious trying to meet such demands. This could be seen in you worrying excessively about getting results or about what you will do afterwards. Not only does it mess with your mind, it could also be affecting your physical health.

What are the symptoms?

- Difficulty getting to sleep or difficulty waking up in the morning
- Constant fatigue
- Forgetfulness
- Aches and pains for no apparent reason
- Poor appetite
- Social withdrawal
- Loss of interest in activities
- Increased anxiety and irritability
- 'Flying off the handle'
- Increased heart rate
- Migraines/headaches
- Blurred vision
- Dizziness

Everyone has bad days but if you've noticed three or more of the above symptoms and you've experienced them for some weeks you may need to do something about your stress levels. Visit your local GP to rule out other possible reasons for the symptoms such as depression. If you think you may be suffering from stress it is worth visiting your GP for a check-up. Stressed-out people have higher blood pressure, and where stress-levels hit boiling point sufferers are at a higher risk of death from any cause than their more chilled-out colleagues. They are also prone to heart disease, colitis (inflammation of the bowels), thyroid disorders, and ulcers.

What causes it?

In the case of exam results time it may be:

- Pressure from parents and relatives to do well
- The need to get high grades to get on track for the career you really want (be it medicine, journalism or mechanics)
- Uncertainty on what to do next – 'There are so many options, what if I make the wrong choice?'
- The whole process of everything changing in your life – friends and yourself maybe moving away, your daily and weekly structure will be totally different

The thing to remember is that while all of these fears and concerns are completely natural (all your mates are probably feeling exactly the same whether they let on or not) if you are getting yourself really worked up you need to try and relax.

How do I deal with it?

If you are suffering from stress try some of the following ways to calm down and chill out:

- Try to make time for yourself away from work to wind down. For example relaxing in a warm bubble bath, listening to soothing music and shutting out the world for a while.
- Take time for your mind and body to relax. Methods can include reading, meditation and yoga.
- Take time to exercise. Regular and frequent exercise is a good stress reducer.
- Eat well, skipping meals will deplete your energy and leave you drained.
- Talk to your family and friends. Make time to see your mates, it will help you unwind and let you unburden any problems.

■ The above information is from TheSite's website which can be found at www.thesite.org

© TheSite.org

Dealing with exam stress

Tips for successful studying

Revising

Exam time is the climax to all your years at school. The pressure to do well can cause stress at exam time and is difficult to handle. Remember that exam time is not the only chance you'll have to prove yourself. Being able to organise your revision time will help to prepare you for when the exams start. Some tips are listed below:

- Write your own revision notes; you will learn as you write. Reading your notes back out loud can help to make what you have written sink in.
- Choose specific areas to study, don't only choose the ones you find easiest but try to challenge yourself.
- Time yourself if you are concerned about only having a short time to answer the questions.
- Don't overdo it. Your concentration will lapse after an hour or so. Give yourself plenty of breaks from your books.
- But avoid temptations. Distractions reduce the flow in your concentration and make it harder to return to your books. Allocate times in the day for relaxing and times for studying.

Under pressure

Feeling as though people are relying on your success at exam time is an added and unnecessary pressure. Talk to your family if they are piling the pressure on. Sometimes people are only keen for you to do well but if their interest is worrying you, discuss it with them. Remember that you can talk to teachers and friends too, if you need some support. Be sure to:

- Set your own goals. Be realistic and make targets that you will be likely to achieve. Try not to live up to others' expectations if you feel they are unrealistic.
- Relax. Take time away from your books. Do something completely

The National Youth Agency

different, have a bath, walk around the block. This will help you to focus when you come back to the revision.

- Try not to miss meals. Taking time out for food will help keep you on top of things.
- Exercise and sports can help to relieve stress and will increase your energy.
- Get some sleep. If you are suffering from insomnia you will feel tired and irritable. It can be reduced if you avoid drinks with a high caffeine content. Instead of coffee, tea and cola late into the night choose water or hot milky drinks.
- Shout for help if you need it. There are plenty of people around to help you when the going is hard.

At exam time

Everyone panics at exam time (even those who say they don't!). Going into one exam still stressed from the last will not help. Go over the positive bits of the last exam and

reassure yourself of the strengths you have. Think about what you will do after it is over. Here are a few practical suggestions:

- Write down the dates and times of each exam and tick them off when they are finished. You will feel a sense of achievement every time an exam is over.
- Break up the time between each one. Mix in the things you like doing with organising your revision time; go shopping and treat yourself, go to the cinema or rent videos, have quiet nights in with friends, get takeaways and wind down.
- Have small celebrations each time an exam is over but save the big party until they are all behind you.

After the exams are over

Give yourself time to relax and get over the exams. Forget about them for as long as you can. Waiting for the results to arrive can also be a stressful time.

If you have been successful, well done. But if you have not done so well, don't panic. There are lots of options. You may be disappointed and find it difficult to think about what to do next. There are lots of people around to help make the decisions with you. You may choose to retake some of the exams, or perhaps take a year out and come back to your studies later.

Don't keep your worries to yourself. Talk to your parents, teachers or friends about how you feel. ChildLine offers help at exam time and you can write to or telephone them at any time. They also have web pages dedicated to helping you through your exams.

■ The above information is from the National Youth Agency's www.youthinformation.com website

© National Youth Agency (NYA)

Stressed students seek medical help

By Joanne Lawson

One in 10 students waiting for A-level results has sought medical attention for stress-related symptoms, according to research from the University of Hertfordshire.

The university interviewed more than 100 students who would be receiving their results the next day. Some 21% of students reported suffering from depression, 12% from insomnia and 8% from panic attacks.

Despite predictions that they will once again outperform boys in exams this year, girls reported more symptoms of stress and anxiety than their male counterparts.

A report by the Association of Teachers and Lecturers in August 2004, found that GCSE and A-level students were suffering from persistent feelings of anxiety and stress due to the constant pressure of exams.

According to Hertfordshire, some of the stress could be relieved if students made back-up plans. Three-quarters of 18-year-olds admitted their stress was heightened because they had little knowledge of the Clearing system. One in 10 said they only heard about the service through a friend.

Alastair McFadyen, head of admissions at the university, said: 'Results time is an incredibly nerve-racking experience and more than four in 10 (42%) school leavers have considered leaving education as a result of not knowing what to do or how to get a university place.

'But there are many avenues available. Options such as the Clearing process often give students a better

Some 21% of students reported suffering from depression, 12% from insomnia and 8% from panic attacks

opportunity of finding the right course and university whether their results are better or worse than expected.'

Earlier this year, the mental health charity Mind released research that showed young people were more likely than any other age group to report feelings of isolation and loneliness.

A spokesman told Education-Guardian.co.uk: 'It is not particularly surprising that A-level students will be experiencing heightened levels of mental distress at a time of increased uncertainty and pressure to perform. But clearly there is a case for paying closer attention to the mental health of Britain's youth.'

ChildLine reported a major rise in calls about exam stress this year and has issued advice to parents and young people of what to do if results were not as good as hoped. 'It is vital to reassure children that there is life after exams, that they are not the only route to success, and that they will still be loved and valued no matter how they perform.'

The charity is also involved in developing peer support networks in schools to help children help each other through stressful exam times.

© *Guardian Newspapers Limited 2004*

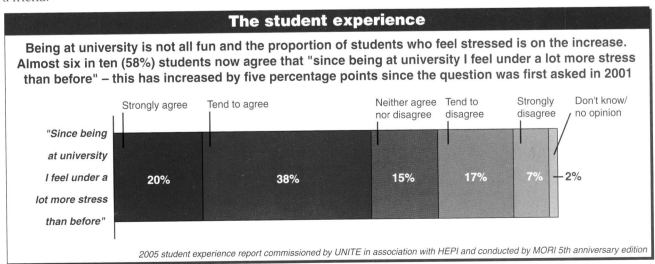

The student experience

Being at university is not all fun and the proportion of students who feel stressed is on the increase. Almost six in ten (58%) students now agree that "since being at university I feel under a lot more stress than before" – this has increased by five percentage points since the question was first asked in 2001

	Strongly agree	Tend to agree	Neither agree nor disagree	Tend to disagree	Strongly disagree	Don't know/ no opinion
"Since being at university I feel under a lot more stress than before"	20%	38%	15%	17%	7%	2%

2005 student experience report commissioned by UNITE in association with HEPI and conducted by MORI 5th anniversary edition

Meditation for children

Could meditation be the key to raising balanced, focused children who perform better both academically and creatively? Anna Selby investigates

Stress became one of those buzz-words of the 1990s, humming its way through the decade as the cause of all ills. At one end of the spectrum we were presented with bloated businessmen suffering heart attacks as they ran for the train, at the other working mothers pulled every which way and reaching for the Prozac. Stress was the bogeyman that would dog you if you had a high-powered job or if you were long-term unemployed, if you were getting divorced or buying a house, or even if you were going on holiday. In fact, it could make just about everyone suffer – except for one significant group: children.

Childhood stress

Most of us would like to think that childhood is a time of happiness and innocence. The reality is that children are under just as much pressure as the rest of us. Exams are now taken by children as young as six and seven – and children are only too aware of the importance of academic performance to most parents. But these are not the only stresses for children. Peer pressure and bullying are rife, more families break up than ever before, and even time off tends to be a relentless bombardment of noise and image in the form of television and computer games. Born into a mercilessly hectic

and noisy world, children may find that the only quiet moments they experience are when they are asleep.

As adults, we have tried some unusual methods of stress-busting. We have suspended ourselves in dark flotation tanks, inhaled flower essences and become addicted to everything from aerobics to re-birthing. However, long-term stress is another matter, manifesting itself as high blood pressure, raised cholesterol levels, anxiety, depression and insomnia.

The seeds of stress

To overcome these problems, a quite different form of deep relaxation is needed, in which severe stress of both body and mind can disperse. Rather

> *Most of us would like to think that childhood is a time of happiness and innocence. The reality is that children are under just as much pressure as the rest of us*

surprisingly – for a practice in which to the observer it appears that nothing much is happening – regular meditation has emerged as the most effective way of achieving this. A considerable body of research – focusing mainly on the most dramatic and measurable manifestations of stress, such as heart disease – has shown it results in substantial reductions in high blood pressure and cholesterol levels. The seeds of these diseases of middle and later life, though, have generally been sown long before we become aware of them. Perhaps even as long ago as childhood.

The authors of *Teaching Meditation to Children*, David Fontana and Ingrid Slack, two psychologists who specialise in working with children, certainly believe so. They suggest that children should be taught to meditate because 'The more we can help children to be at peace with their own bodies, the better chance we have of helping them avoid these killers in later life.' The benefits, however, are not just for the future.

The benefits

Meditation gives even very young children power over their thinking and their emotions, not by a repressive self-control, but by enhanced self-understanding and

self-acceptance. Fontana and Slack advocate meditation as a gentle and effective means of overcoming a wide variety of psychological and behavioural problems, such as anxiety, hyperactivity and aggression, and they back this up with case histories. They also see meditation as a much more general tool, applicable to all children and bringing the following benefits:

- Physical relaxation
- Improved concentration
- Increased tranquillity and ability to deal with stress
- Improved awareness
- Improved creativity
- Improved memory

Transcendental Meditation

At the moment, the concept of children meditating is still in its infancy. One of the few places where children can learn is with Transcendental Meditation. If the Maharishi conjures images of the Beatles, beads and kaftans, you might be surprised to learn that one of TM's most vociferous advocates these days is retired chairman of ICI, Sir John Harvey-Jones. He believes its stress-busting powers make it vital for anyone working in business. Over four million people have now learned the technique worldwide – and technique is the relevant word here. Adherents point out that it is, in essence, a mind exercise. Religious beliefs are irrelevant and, once you have been trained to meditate, you practise the technique alone, so no further involvement with the TM organisation is necessary.

For adults, the technique consists of mentally repeating a mantra twice a day for 20 minutes. Effortlessness is emphasised – it doesn't matter if you are constantly distracted by thoughts or even if you fall asleep. You just go back to the mantra when you realise you're not saying it any more. For young children, it is different, because it is not considered advisable for children to sit for any length of time with their eyes closed – even if they could. Instead they do it as they walk to school or play with Lego. At five they 'do their word' for five minutes twice a day and thereafter add one minute for each year of their age.

Meditation at school

So far, there is only one school in the country where meditation forms part of the curriculum – the Maharishi School in Skelmersdale in Lancashire. Started in 1986 by a group of dissatisfied parents (all meditators), the school began with one teacher and 14 children. There are now 100 children, ranging from four-year-olds in the reception class to 16-year-olds taking GCSEs.

If the effectiveness of meditation is measured in terms of academic success alone, the school results would seem pretty conclusive: for four out of the last five years, the Maharishi School has been top of the Lancashire league table for GCSE results. It is also in the top 2.5 per cent of the schools in the country, including the top selective independent schools. This performance is even more remarkable as the school is not academically selective and is happy to take children who have not fared well in other schools.

Creatively, they are thriving, too: pupils at the school have now won so many poetry competitions that they're currently under a one-win-a-term rule from the Poetry Society. Clearly, something is working but is it meditation?

Focusing on balance

Derek Cassells, the headmaster, certainly thinks meditation is the key and, interestingly, he regards stress as the underlying cause of all learning and behavioural problems. 'We have a very traditional curriculum but, because we also have TM or word of wisdom for the younger children, they experience a level of rest that is at least twice as

deep as deep sleep, twice every day. Stresses and tensions are released and the nervous system is brought into balance. From that balance come all the benefits – such as greater ability to focus – and this produces academic results. These aren't our goal; they're just a side effect. What's important is that the children are so at ease they automatically enjoy learning and they can utilise more of their potential. We just bring out what's already there.'

The teachers all meditate, too. The maths teacher, Mark Gaskell, says, 'If I closed my eyes – as we do every day during meditation – in most schools, when I opened them again, the class wouldn't be there. After this deep silence, the children are very aware, alert and receptive. This is the great benefit for a teacher. In other schools, it's a struggle just to get the class to be quiet and listen, let alone teach them something. Here, they're refreshed and happy. It's easier for them to be creative because they want to learn.' The theory is that there is an underlying association between brainwave coherence (brainwaves becoming more synchronised between the hemispheres of the brain during meditation) and learning and creative thought.

Understandably delighted with all this success, Derek Cassells is now keen to encourage other schools to take up meditation. 'People are looking for a better system of education. Extra cramming and more pressure are finally being recognised as the wrong approach and there is more willingness to consider something different. We have been talking to a range of schools who are interested in using our methods.'

Children with learning difficulties

Keith Snape teaches at one such school that specialises in pupils with learning difficulties. Still in the early stages of introducing meditation to a few of the children, the school isn't ready to officially 'go public', but teachers, pupils and parents all claim to have already seen positive results.

Such schools are, of course, rare exceptions, while the pressures put on children continue to soar.

'Unhappily, little is done within formal education to help [children] learn to understand themselves, to control their anxieties and their thought processes and to discover tranquillity, harmony and balance within themselves,' say authors David Fontana and Ingrid Slack.

'Little is done to help them to manage their own inner lives, to use their mental energy productively instead of dissipating it in worries and random thinking, and to access the creative levels of their own minds. Meditation is one of the most important ways in which we can help young children cope better with their lives, at both the personal and the academic levels.'

Activities for children

There are teachers of Transcendental Meditation all over the country or, if you'd like to try introducing meditation to your child yourself, here are a few ideas to help you get started:

Breathing meditation

This is a good basic meditation for adults and children alike but, while adults can practise it for 20 minutes or more, young children should do it for no more than five minutes, and only one or two to start with. This is a very calming meditation as it slows down the breathing – we breathe more quickly and shallowly when anxious – and it helps the body to relax, too.

You can do this in a chair, providing your feet are flat on the floor, but children prefer to sit cross-

> *'Unhappily, little is done within formal education to help children learn to understand themselves, to control their anxieties and their thought processes'*

legged on the floor. Make sure they are sitting on a cushion, their backs are straight and they have closed eyes. Then guide the meditation as follows:

Become aware of your breathing. Focus upon the feeling of coolness at your nose when you breathe in and the feeling of warmth as you breathe out. Don't let your attention follow the breath into your lungs. Pretend you're a sentry who is on guard at that point, watching carefully everything that goes in and out of the gates of the city. If thoughts try to get in the way, look upon them simply as people trying to distract you and take no notice of them.

Later, you can introduce counting the breaths.

Kinhin

This is a walking meditation from Zen Buddhism and particularly useful for children who find it hard to stay still for the previous meditation. It is rather like moving in slow motion and with the utmost care. Choose a path or a straight line for the children to walk along and ask them to lift

one foot at a time slowly and very carefully feeling every muscle used in the process and every shift in body weight. The foot is placed smoothly and slowly the same distance ahead and then a step is taken with the other foot. Children usually love this and it brings great body awareness.

'A Safe Place'

This is an excellent meditation when children are feeling stressed or anxious. Begin with a minute or two of the breathing meditation and then talk them through every part of their bodies, asking them to check that it is relaxed – from their toes through their legs, backs, stomachs, shoulders, necks, faces and scalps.

Now ask them to picture in their minds a peaceful place. This can be somewhere they know or an imagined place, it is completely up to them. Tell them to go into this place and sit down (in their minds) and look all around them to see all of the things they like and enjoy. Explain that this is a place they can always go to where they know they can feel safe and relaxed.

Give them a few minutes to enjoy the sensation and then bring them back to the room and their breathing for a minute or two. Then ask them to open their eyes and remind them that this is their special place, always there for them in their own minds.

■ The above article is reproduced with kind permission from www.ivillage.co.uk

Stress and the workforce

Stress becomes the No 1 complaint of British workers. Survey warns of high pressures in public and private sectors

Stress is the biggest threat to the health of the nation's workforce, according to a survey published in October 2004 highlighting Britain's gruelling office culture.

Anxiety over heavy workloads, long hours and the threat of redundancy is fuelling an epidemic of stress, with 58 per cent of union health and safety representatives citing it as the major cause of complaints – outstripping conditions such as back pain and repetitive strain injury.

The findings published by the TUC, will prompt a fresh debate over whether modern office life really is more pressured – or whether the rise in 'stress' complaints reflects the decline of more acute physical dangers in the workplace.

Stress at work is estimated to cost the economy £7 billion a year in sick pay, lost productivity and NHS bills.

Brendan Barber, TUC general secretary, said the levels of stress uncovered by the report suggested the drive to help people juggle work and family was not delivering. 'We know that long hours and dense workloads are stressful. We know that workers want a better work-life balance, yet some employers insist on trying to squeeze every last drop of sweat out of their workforce,' he said.

Stressed employees were likely to be demoralised and less productive, he said, and it was in employers' interests to relieve them.

The Health and Safety Executive is expected to publish new guidelines on stress, warning employers to protect their staff by auditing stress levels and offering counselling.

The TUC survey of almost 5,000

By Gaby Hinsliff, Chief Political Correspondent

health and safety staff found public sector workers were more likely than those in the private sector to complain of stress. Although being overloaded with work was the most common cause, there was a slight rise in complaints of stress due to redundancies. The findings come as civil servants are due to strike in protest against plans for thousands of Whitehall redundancies.

Professor Cary Cooper, an international expert on stress, said

Stress levels at work

Factors linked to overwork or stress

Factor	Percentage
Workloads	79%
Cuts in staff	49%
Change	47%
Long hours	37%
Bullying	27%
Shiftwork	22%
Cramped working conditions	17%
Redundancies	14%
Sex or racial discrimination	3%

4,521 health and safety representatives completed the questionnaire online or by post during the late spring and summer 2004.

Source: Trades Union Congress (TUC)

the findings reflected the 'Americanisation' of the British workplace.

'Jobs are no longer for life, you have the longest working hours in Europe, you have major social changes over the past 15 years – two out of three families are now [both parents] working – and we have cut labour costs,' he said. 'We have become too lean and mean, we have employed as few people as possible to make us as competitive as possible.'

He said public sector workers had repeatedly been found to show more stress than colleagues in the commercial world, despite the common perception that they enjoyed shorter hours and a less cutthroat atmosphere.

'There is constant change in the public sector, because it's influenced by the government – whoever is in government, not just this one,' he added.

However, some argue that stress is a convenient way of describing a mix of entirely normal emotions, from boredom and frustration to unhappiness and fatigue.

Frank Furedi, head of sociology at Kent University and the author of a recent book critical of Britain's 'therapy culture', has warned of a growing industry of stress-managers, life coaches and gurus who generate business by promoting a sense of insecurity and inability to cope. Research has shown that some short-lived stress can have positive health benefits.

Yet stress, anxiety and depression are the biggest triggers of new claims for incapacity benefit from people saying they are too sick to work, and employers have warned of a rise in employment tribunal claims involving alleged stress-related illness.

Cooper said: 'Pressure can be healthy, stimulating and motivating, but when it exceeds an individual's ability to cope, then you have stress.'

Signs of stress

- loss of concentration
- loss of motivation
- increased irritability
- increased sensitivity to criticism
- difficulty sleeping
- waking early
- nail-biting
- smoking or drinking more
- indigestion

Work stress triggers

- insecurity and the threat of unemployment
- feeling undervalued

- poor working conditions
- too much or too little to do
- lack of communication
- an unsupportive boss
- too much pressure
- bad relationships with colleagues
- work that is too difficult or not challenging enough
- lack of control over the way your work is done
- interference in private life

■ This article first appeared in *The Observer*, 31 October 2004.

Stressful careers

Teachers and social workers top league of stressful careers

Teaching and social work have been ranked as the most stressful professions, according to new research.

The occupations gained the dubious distinctions of appearing in the top three for both poor psychological wellbeing and physical ill health caused by stress.

Occupational psychologists also concluded that 'emotional labour' involving face-to-face or telephone contact with clients, and sometimes the suppressing of emotions, was a central factor in what makes a job stressful.

Other professions also found to involve high levels of stress were ambulance service employees, call centre staff, prison officers, clerical and administrative staff and police officers.

The results of a major study of more than 25,000 employees in 24 occupations were presented to delegates at the British Psychological Society's Division of Occupational Psychology annual conference being held at Warwick.

Sheena Johnson, a psychology researcher at the University of Liverpool and one of those behind the study, said: 'This is the first time we have been able to comprehensively compare so many different occupations.

'We found that seven of the occupations scored worse then

By Nic Fleming, Science Correspondent

average for both psychological wellbeing and physical health as a result of stress. Of these, six were ones that were rated as having a high degree of emotional labour.

'These are people whose work involves a lot of face-to-face or telephone contact. They are likely to be having to hide or not express their emotions. We set out to test the view that emotional labour is an important facet of the experience of occupational stress and found that to be correct.'

The three professions that scored worst for physical ill health related to work stress were ambulance service employees, teachers and social workers

Previous studies have identified teachers, healthcare professionals, social workers and ambulance service employees as suffering particularly high levels of stress at work, and have also identified emotional labour

as being an important component of a stressful job.

However, no previous work has compared the emotional content of so many different occupations and examined the degree to which this makes them stressful.

Mrs Johnson and other researchers collected data on stress levels from 25,352 employees working in 24 different occupations and ranked their averages according to two measures.

The three professions that scored worst for physical ill health related to work stress were ambulance service employees, teachers and social workers.

They were followed by call centre workers, bar staff and prison officers. Social workers, teachers and firefighters scored lowest for psychological wellbeing, followed by ambulance service workers, vets and lecturers.

Eight experts were asked to rate the occupations as having high, average or low emotional content.

The seven identified as having worse than average rankings for both physical ill health related to work stress and psychological wellbeing were ambulance service employees, teachers, social workers, call centre staff, prison officers, clerical and administrative staff and police officers.

Stressed out

Summary results of a Mori Omnibus Survey carried out on behalf of Samaritans

The results of this year's survey when compared to last year's show that stress levels are probably increasing slightly. The majority of people experience some level of stress (82%), and a significant minority experience high levels of stress. There are clear regional variations in people's responses, and age plays a crucial role in perception of stress.

■ 20% get stressed on a daily basis (one in five) – i.e. most of the time. This is an increase of 4% of people on last year.

■ 23% are stressed more than once a week (over one-third of the UK), but not every day.

■ The majority of the population (62%) is stressed out at least once a month or more.

■ Men and women suffer from roughly the same levels of stress, regardless of how much stress they suffer from – none, some, a lot.

■ 23% of people working full time get stressed every day compared to just 16% of those who aren't working.

■ Young people are the most stressed out on a daily basis, with 24% of those aged 15-24 getting wound up every day.

■ By contrast, older Britons aged 55+ are a lot more chilled out with only 12% claiming to get stressed daily.

■ Money seems to make little difference to stress levels: those with a household income of less than £17k experience similar stress levels to those whose household income is more than £30k.

■ Parents are significantly more stressed than the average Briton – with nearly one-third (29%) experiencing stress at least once a day compared to one-fifth on average.

■ 18% of the population is completely laid back, claiming never to suffer from stress.

■ East Midlands, London, the North East, and South West regions are the regions that suffer most often from daily stress, with nearly one in four (24%) becoming stressed out at least once a day.

■ As well as daily stress, the North East also had the highest proportion of people who never got stressed – nearly one-third, 29% said they never get stressed.

The results of question two provide evidence that people believe that they are more stressed than five years ago – the majority of people are experiencing similar or greater levels of stress than five years ago. Responses varied considerably by age, suggesting that stress, and the perception of stress, changes as time goes on. There are no marked differences between how men and women feel about their stress levels compared to five years ago and there is limited regional variation.

■ Two out of five people are more stressed than they were five years ago (40%).

■ Over half of those between the ages of 15 and 34 are more stressed than they were five years ago (53%).

■ Just under half of all those below the age of 54 are more stressed than they were five years ago, whilst less than a quarter of those above the age of 55 are more stressed, suggesting stress levels peak in middle age and then begin to subside as people approach retirement.

■ Women were slightly more likely to say that their stress levels have increased in the past five years compared to men – 42% of women compared to 38% of men.

■ People's stress levels are increasing most in the West Midlands, with nearly half the population (49%) saying they felt more stressed.

■ Unsurprisingly, those who said they were most stressed (on a daily basis) are also those whose stress levels have risen most in the past five years (68%).

■ The above information is from the Samaritans' website which can be found at www.samaritans.org.uk

© Samaritans

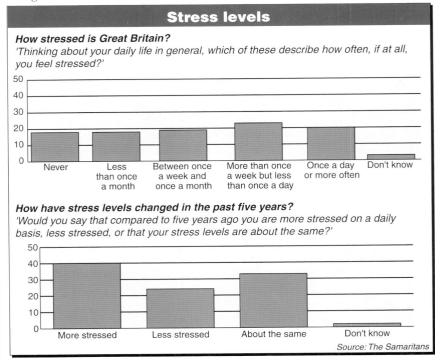

Stress levels

How stressed is Great Britain?
'Thinking about your daily life in general, which of these describe how often, if at all, you feel stressed?'

How have stress levels changed in the past five years?
'Would you say that compared to five years ago you are more stressed on a daily basis, less stressed, or that your stress levels are about the same?'

Source: The Samaritans

Stress and bullying

Success Unlimited

'There's only one way of dealing with stress – that's to identify the cause and then work to reduce or eliminate that cause. I believe bullying is the main, but least recognised, cause of stress in the workplace today.'

Tim Field

'Poor management is a major cause of stress.'

Dr Peter Graham, Head of Health Directorate, UK Health & Safety Executive, 24 September 1998

Stress is not the employee's inability to cope with excessive workloads and the unreasonable demands of incompetent and bullying managers; stress is a consequence of the employer's failure to provide a safe system of work as required by the UK Health & Safety at Work Act 1974. Blaming the sufferer of stress for suffering stress is an admission of failure to fulfil this obligation of duty of care.

The HSE publication *Working on Stress* describes the view that 'All you need to do is go for counselling to stop work-related stress' as 'wrong' and as being 'unlikely to tackle the source of the problem'.

HSE Stress Management Standards

Stress comes in two forms: positive and negative

Positive stress (or eustress) is the result of competent management and mature leadership where everyone works together and everyone is valued and supported. Positive stress enhances well-being and can be harnessed to enhance performance and fuel achievement.

Negative stress (or distress) is the result of a bullying climate where threat, coercion and fear substitute for non-existent management skills. Employees have to work twice as hard to achieve half as much to compensate for the dysfunctional and inefficient management. Negative stress diminishes quality of life and

causes injury to health resulting in the symptoms of ill-health. When people use the word 'stress' on its own, they usually mean 'negative stress'. The CBI estimates stress and stress-related illness cost UK industry and taxpayers £12 billion each year. The UK Department of Health state that 3.6% of national average salary budget is paid to employees off sick with stress. Stress is now officially the Number One cause of sickness absence although 20% of employers still do not regard stress as a health and safety issue.

Fight or flight: the stress response

The fight or flight mechanism, or stress response, is designed for responding to physical danger (e.g. being about to be attacked by a sabre-toothed tiger) but today is more likely to be activated by a psychological

---

The CBI estimates stress and stress-related illness cost UK industry and taxpayers £12 billion each year

---

danger (e.g. bullying at work, harassment, stalking, abuse) for which it was not designed. The stress response can also be activated by anticipation of low-probability or long-term or non-life-threatening events such as financial problems (clinching the next big deal, how to pay the mortgage next month, wondering when the next benefit cheque will arrive), motorway traffic jams, job security, picking up a parking ticket for a car park overstay, etc.

Different people respond with different degrees of stress to different stressors, a fact which has dogged research. However, there are at least four factors which determine the degree to which one will feel stressed:

- control: a person feels stressed to the extent to which they perceive they are not in control of the stressor; at work, employees have no control over their management
- predictability: a person feels stressed to the extent to which they are unable to predict the behaviour or occurrence of the stressor (bullies are notoriously unpredictable in their behaviour)
- expectation: a person feels stressed to the extent to which they perceive their circumstances are

www.independence.co.uk

not improving and will not improve (a bullying situation almost always gets worse, especially as one gains insight into the cause)

■ support: a person feels stressed to the extent to which they lack support systems, including work colleagues, management, personnel, union, partner, family, friends, colleagues, persons in authority, official bodies, professionals, and the law

Once the stress response is activated, the body's energy is diverted to where it is needed, thus heart rate, blood pressure and breathing rate increase. All non-essential body functions are temporarily shut down or operate at reduced level; these include digestion, growth, sexual systems (menstrual cycle, libido, testosterone production), immune system, storage of energy as fat, etc. In response to threat, glucose, proteins and fats are

> *Once the stress response is activated, the body's energy is diverted to where it is needed, thus heart rate, blood pressure and breathing rate increase*

rapidly released from storage (in muscles, fat cells and liver) and energy becomes abundantly available to those muscles which will help you fight the danger or run away from it. In extreme cases bowels and bladder will spontaneously evacuate to lighten the load; the smell may also help to deter the attacker. There is no point in digestion, reproduction and immune system etc. continuing to operate if you're likely to be the

sabre-toothed tiger's dinner in the next ten minutes – better divert that energy into avoiding being on the menu.

Therefore, the prospect of going to work, or the thought or sound of the bully approaching immediately activates the stress response, but fighting or flight are both inappropriate. In repeated bullying, the stress response prepares the body to respond physically when what is required is an employer-wide anti-bullying policy, knowledge of bullying motivations and tactics, assertive responses to defend ourselves against unwarranted verbal and physical harassment, and effective laws against bullying as an ultimate deterrent or arbiter when all else fails.

■ The above information is from Success Unlimited's website which can be found at www.bullyonline.org

© *Success Unlimited*

Common causes of stress

Information from Work Positive

Sickness absence

Sickness absence figures can be systematically recorded and trends monitored in order to establish the causes of absence. Is there a generally high level of absence? Are there variations across departments and are there any cases of long-term absence caused by stress? Assess whether the absence levels are 'normal' for your kind of organisation.

High staff turnover

Conduct exit interviews to establish why people are leaving and take action appropriately. Try to replace staff quickly or provide temporary resources, if necessary, to reduce the increased workload on remaining staff.

Poor communication between teams

Try to establish open forums for communication of information, such as team meetings, group meetings, etc. Look at the systems in place for

top-down communication (e.g. company policy, performance, etc.), bottom-up communication (feedback from staff, involvement of staff in decision making) and cross-functional communication (between colleagues/teams). Are these means of communication effective for the type of information that is being communicated? It may be helpful to set up a group to review the current systems, types of information to be communicated and the most appropriate means of communication for each.

Bullying

Provide training for the staff involved to improve interpersonal skills. Establish a formal bullying and violence policy to communicate the seriousness of such inappropriate behaviour. Establish and communicate avenues for reporting bullying.

Lack of feedback on performance

Establish an appropriate performance management system with performance indicators that are agreed in consultation with employees. Make sure it is a two-way process including positive feedback on performance, areas for improvement, future goals and objectives, training needs, and any other issues. Include performance review as a performance indicator for staff managers to communicate the importance of the procedure. Feedback on performance should not be restricted to performance reviews. Try to instil a culture of positive feedback across the workforce.

Value and contribution

If people feel undervalued it may be that their contribution to the business is not recognised. This is often associated with lack of feedback on performance. Try to instil a culture whereby all staff acknowledge the contribution of their colleagues. Managers should lead by example in this by providing informal feedback to employees on a regular basis.

Technological change

If there has been new technology introduced, check that staff are comfortable with its use; are there any problems associated with it? Provide refresher training as an option.

Lack of clarity of roles and responsibilities

Review current roles and responsibilities. If current roles are appropriate, clarify these by producing job descriptions. These should be conducted in conjunction with staff and made available to all staff. If they are not appropriate, establish revised roles in consultation with staff.

Dissatisfaction with non-monetary benefits

Re-assess non-monetary benefits such as holidays, flexible hours, Christmas bonus, etc. Often token benefits that do not cost very much can be much appreciated, e.g. increased holiday entitlement with service, shopping vouchers as

---

Remember that you may be required by law to look at specific aspects of the work environment, such as noise, computer workstations, lighting, hazardous substances, etc.

Christmas bonus, more flexible working hours, subsidised access to local leisure facilities, etc.

Working long hours

Monitor the hours that are being worked by staff. Is workload evenly distributed? Is there a culture of working late, is this necessary to get the job done? Can the work be rationalised or can temporary staff be brought in during peaks of high workload to support permanent staff during these times?

Boring and mundane work

Is it possible to rotate jobs so that people are not doing the same job all the time? A workforce that is 'multi-skilled' is more flexible.

One-off incidents

If there have been one-off incidents that have caused stress in the past, analyse them to identify whether they were managed well. What could have been done differently to reduce pressure on staff?

Uncomfortable workplace

Consult employees about the workplace and why they are not happy with the working environment. Small changes can have a big impact, particularly if employees have control over the way that it is set out and are involved in choosing equipment, furniture, etc. Remember that you may be required by law to look at specific aspects of the work environment, such as noise, computer workstations, lighting, hazardous substances, etc.

Lack of training

Establish a system for identifying training needs. This may be simply asking staff if they feel that they require training to improve their performance. Remember to do this for all staff. Identify the priority areas and communicate these to all staff, explaining why these have been chosen as priority areas.

■ Work Positive has been developed by NHS Health Scotland, Health and Safety Authority Ireland, Health and Safety Executive GB to help organisations address this very important health and safety issue – stress at work. For more information visit www.workpositive.co.uk

© NHS Health Scotland, Health and Safety Authority Ireland, Health and Safety Executive GB.

Suffering in silence

A quarter of the UK population fight a daily battle with mental health problems. Work can be the cause as well as a means of coping with this most debilitating of illnesses

By Erika Lucas

Mental health is one of society's last taboos. The whole subject is surrounded by myth and – thanks to media misrepresentation – is widely misunderstood. It probably isn't even on your organisation's radar screen – but it certainly should be.

Research shows that one in four people will experience some kind of mental health problem in any one year. That means that someone sitting next to you now may well be suffering from severe stress, manic depression or some kind of obsessive or compulsive disorder. Such is the stigma surrounding these conditions, that the likelihood is you will never know your colleague even has a problem. They will suffer in silence, descending into a downward spiral – afraid that if they speak up and ask for help, they will be ridiculed or may even lose their job.

Of course there can be a whole raft of triggers behind an episode of poor mental health – but work-related pressure is often a major contributory factor and poor management practice can exacerbate the situation. UK plc needs to sit up and take notice, because the cost to industry is huge. Over 91 million working days are lost each year due to mental ill health, at an estimated cost to industry of £4 billion.

The good news, however, is that the majority of mental illnesses are entirely treatable and if properly supported, people can make a full recovery. So what can organisations do to provide mentally healthy workplaces and a supportive environment for staff who are suffering?

According to Alison Cobb of mental health charity Mind, developing a clear policy on employment and mental health is a good start. Employers have an obligation under the Disability Discrimination Act to make sure they treat people with mental health problems fairly. New Health and Safety Executive (HSE) standards also require them to assess the risk of work-related stress and take measures to control it within their organisation.

So existing employment and equal opportunities policies need to be reviewed and adapted to make sure they encompass people with mental health problems. Senior level commitment is vital, says Cobb, adding that it is good practice to also involve staff from across the business in the development of a mental health policy.

> *UK plc needs to sit up and take notice, because the cost to industry is huge. Over 91 million working days are lost each year due to mental ill health, at an estimated cost to industry of £4 billion*

Mental health specialist Peter Christison stresses, however, that pinning a policy up on the wall isn't enough. Organisations need to educate their staff about mental ill-health and create a supportive culture where sufferers can discuss their problems openly and without fear of discrimination.

'Putting a notice up on the board is only tinkering with the issue,' he says. 'It has to be done in a demonstrative way so that people can see there is a social fabric where someone with mental illness is treated in the same way as someone who has a physical illness or has broken their leg skiing.'

Organisations also need to put their working practices under the microscope and make sure they are not encouraging unhealthy long-hours cultures and inappropriate management behaviour.

Research from the Depression Alliance has shown that unrealistic workloads and bad management are one of the major contributors to the growing incidence of depression.

'Factors that might act as a trigger are when people have competing demands and prioritisation is impossible because everything becomes a deadline,' says Christison. 'Role conflicts, where people are perhaps working for two managers, or a poor balance between effort and reward can also exacerbate the problem.'

Christison's consultancy run 'Healthy Minds in the Workplace', a training programme that helps organisations make the necessary shift in mindset. Managers receive advice on creating a mentally healthy environment, and learn how to recognise some of the signs and symptoms of mental illness. The emphasis is not on turning managers into DIY psychiatrists – but teaching them to be sensitive to changes in people's demeanour or behaviour that may indicate there is a problem.

Typical signs might include someone who is normally punctual turning into a poor time-keeper, or a usually gregarious person becoming withdrawn. An easy-going employee who suddenly becomes irritable or tearful, or someone whose performance takes an inexplicable downturn, may also be showing signs of mental ill-health.

Managers are often unsure about how to deal with someone they suspect may have a problem. If the working relationship is good and there is an open culture within the business, the individual may well feel they can come forward and raise the issue themselves. But if this doesn't happen, the advice is that managers should make sensitive attempts to start a dialogue. 'It's often as simple as saying to the person "I don't want to pry, but you don't seem to be your normal self and I am a bit worried about you," says Christison.

Armed with information about the problem, the manager can then look at what support they may be able to provide. This will vary according to individual needs, but might mean redesigning the person's role, making adjustments to specific tasks, reducing working hours or encouraging the employee to seek help from one of the supportive agencies.

There is overwhelming evidence that keeping people in work if at all possible is by far the best approach. Having a job to go to helps the individual regain self-esteem and confidence and gives them a purpose – and of course the organisation gets to retain the services of a valuable employee. Research has shown that if a person is absent from work for three months the likelihood they will return is diminished. After six months, it is highly unlikely they will ever come back.

One approach that is growing in popularity is the use of mental health case workers, who support both the organisation and the individual throughout the period of illness. Case workers typically facilitate communication between employer and employee on issues like adjustments to the job or time off work and act as a central point of contact between the company and medical professionals.

They can also act as an advocate for the employee within the organisation, provide training for managers and help employers ensure they are meeting their legal obligations.

'When you look at the number of agencies and people who can be involved, it is easy to see how difficult it is for a person to successfully return to work without a case manager working alongside them,' says mental health specialist Roger

---

'Many people with mental health problems do want to work, yet fewer than a quarter actually do'

Butterworth. 'People can make precipitous decisions, like resigning because they feel they have "let the side down". They may enter into conflict situations with line managers and work colleagues, or they may fall out with their spouses who are trying to help but don't know how.'

Butterworth has recently completed a government-funded pilot project on job retention support for people with mental health problems. This is part of a wider, national drive to end the stigma associated with mental health and provide better support for people who want to stay in work.

The £2.7 million programme includes improved training on mental health issues for job centre staff, more support, advice and training for employers, and funding for people with mental health problems who are interested in enterprise and self-employment.

'Many people with mental health problems do want to work, yet fewer than a quarter actually do. They are nearly three times as likely to be in debt and more likely to live alone and in poorly-maintained accommodation. The government is determined to address these inequalities,' said Minister for Social Exclusion Jeff Rooker.

Checklist – better mental health at work (courtesy of Mind)

If someone with a mental health problem applies for a job with you:
- Don't make assumptions about their ability
- Don't be afraid to talk about the issue in a constructive way
- Don't discriminate

If a member of staff is showing signs of mental ill health:
- Talk to them about it
- Make sure they know about any support the organisation offers
- Consider the need for adjustments

If you want to develop an equal opportunity policy on mental health:
- Gain commitment at senior level in the organisation
- Review existing equal opportunities policies and procedures, and adapt them to include people with mental health problems
- Involve a range of staff in this process and consider drawing on the expertise of a mental health organisation.

If you want to promote positive mental health throughout your organisation:
- Focus on the quality of management and communication
- Consult with staff about how they rate the quality of the work environment and practices
- Carry out a stress risk assessment
- Develop an action plan
- Display and promote information that encourages employees to look after their mental wellbeing.

- The above article is reproduced by kind permission of *Professional Manager*, published by the Chartered Management Institute, the leading organisation for managers in the UK. Information about *Professional Manager* can be found at www.managers.org.uk/ professionalmanager

© *Chartered Management Institute*

Stress keeps four in ten awake at night

Four out of 10 Britons are spending sleepless nights worrying about their work or home life, a survey shows.

Increased pressure in the workplace and the home are causing growing numbers of adults to suffer anxiety and have problems sleeping, according to the PruHealth Index.

And for 12% of Britons – equivalent to 5.6 million people – sleepless and stress-filled nights were a regular occurrence.

Higher rates among women

The figures were revealed in the PruHealth report, which looked at a variety of health-related topics, including diet, smoking and stress.

The survey of more than 2,000 people found that frequent worrying was twice as common in women as men – 16% compared to 8%.

Younger people were also more commonly afflicted, with 13% of 16-24-year-olds worrying frequently compared to 7% of those aged over 65.

Prof Simon Capewell from the University of Liverpool, who analysed the findings, said: 'These data are consistent with previous surveys showing surprisingly high levels of anxiety and depression in the general population.

'Women have higher levels than men and present more frequently to their GPs.

'Some men try and deny or conceal it.'

Only 14% of workers said they believed their employer took a lot of interest in their health, while 26% described their level of interest as 'reasonable'.

Looking at smoking, the survey found that 27% of adults smoked, with one in three describing themselves as heavy smokers.

The survey of more than 2,000 people found that frequent worrying was twice as common in women as men – 16% compared to 8%

Half of heavy smokers – around 2.4 million people – said they would try to quit in the next year, along with a further four million occasional or social smokers.

Diet and fitness

There was also a mixed result on diet. Half of people who said they ate plenty of fresh fruit and vegetables also confessed to undoing the good work with ready meals, fizzy drinks, sweets and biscuits.

Only 42% of those questioned said they tried to exercise several times a week, while 43% said they did no exercise at all or just once or twice a month.

Prof Capewell said: 'Exercise halves the chances of cardiovascular disease, reduces future risks of osteoporosis and improves mental well-being.

'This need not necessarily be a marathon or competitive sports.

'For many people, simply walking to school or work, or cycling instead of driving would suffice.'

He added: 'The UK has one of the highest rates of disease in Europe, particularly heart disease, stroke and the major cancers.

'These diseases are preventable through healthier lifestyles and healthier environments.

'The recent Government Public Health White Paper has now prioritised prevention, so information on trends in people's health behaviour becomes increasingly valuable.'

■ This article first appeared in *The Daily Mail*, 6 January 2005.
© 2005 Associated Newspapers Ltd

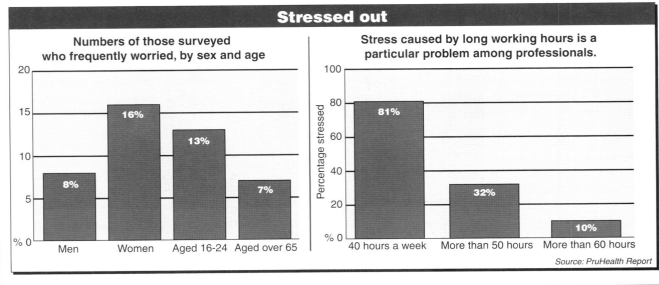

Stressed out

Numbers of those surveyed who frequently worried, by sex and age

- Men: 8%
- Women: 16%
- Aged 16-24: 13%
- Aged over 65: 7%

Stress caused by long working hours is a particular problem among professionals.

Percentage stressed

- 40 hours a week: 81%
- More than 50 hours: 32%
- More than 60 hours: 10%

Source: PruHealth Report

Anxiety attack

As the law on work-related stress shapes up, employers need to take more steps to prevent it – and keep staff informed and involved

By Sarah Empson

Each new case of work-related stress leads to an average of 29 days off work. The Health and Safety Executive estimates that 13.4 million working days were lost to stress and anxiety in 2001.

The HSE defines stress as an adverse reaction to 'excessive pressures or other types of demand'. The reaction can take many forms, and stress has been linked to mental illness, heart disease, back pain, headaches, gastro-intestinal disturbances and alcohol and drug dependency.

A stress claim is usually made up of one or more of the following: a personal injury/negligence claim for damages in the civil courts, a constructive dismissal claim, or a disability discrimination claim in employment tribunals.

Disability under the Disability Discrimination Act 1995 is a physical or mental impairment that has a 'substantial and long term' effect on 'normal day-to-day activities'. At the moment, only an illness lasting more than a year will count. The courts have said mental disability must be a 'clinically well-recognised mental illness', and chronic fatigue syndrome (ME), post-traumatic stress disorder and depression have all been held by tribunals to be disabilities. Stress alone, though, is unlikely to be.

Things are still moving in this area. Recently the government announced changes to its disability discrimination bill, including removing the requirement for a mental illness to be clinically well-recognised. This followed concerns expressed by a parliamentary committee and the charity Mind that people with mental illness were not well served by the law. The changes mean tribunals will focus more on the effects of mental illness and less on how it is labelled; this is likely to lead to more claims for disability discrimination of this sort.

In the meantime, organisations should do what they can to minimise the risk. They should maintain a formal stress policy and ensure all stress-related claims are treated seriously and investigated fully.

Last month, the HSE launched the final version of its new management standards to help employers and employees to prevent stress at work. The standards do not represent law but following them can help employers to meet their legal duties.

Acas has published an advisory booklet, *Stress at work*, to accompany the standards. It provides advice on the causes of stress and policies and training to prevent it, and suggests how employers and employees can work together to tackle the problem. It says organisations should focus on:

- demand – pay attention to job design, employees' training needs and the possibilities of flexible working;
- control – involve employees in day-to-day decision-making;
- support – give employees the opportunity to talk about stress-causing issues, and keep them informed about the outcome;
- relationships – review policies for handling grievances, unsatisfactory performance, poor attendance, misconduct, bullying and harassment;
- role – work out accurate job descriptions and check employees are clear about what's expected of them;
- change – plan ahead so change doesn't come out of the blue; work with employees to solve problems.

Take the strain

The way courts deal with work-related stress claims has been evolving since the first well-publicised case, *Walker v Northumberland County Council* (1995 ICR 702; QBD). Here, the High Court said employers had a duty not to cause employees psychiatric damage by giving them too much work or insufficient support. Damages were reportedly agreed at £175,000.

In *Barber v Somerset County Council* (2004 UKHL 13; HL), the House of Lords said employers had to take the initiative, rather than 'wait and see' as the Court of Appeal suggested. The Lords confirmed this in *Simmons v British Steel* (2004 ICR 585; HL), saying that, while physical injury had to be reasonably foreseeable for employers to be liable, it was not essential for psychiatric injury to be. Employers must deal with an employee's condition when they become aware of it.

■ Sarah Empson is a solicitor in Steeles' employment team.

■ The above article first appeared in *People Management* magazine, 23 December 2004, produced by the Chartered Institute of Personnel and Development (CIPD). For more information visit their websites: www.cipd.co.uk and www.peoplemanagement.co.uk

Anxiety and stress

According to MIND '45 million working days are lost each year through anxiety and stress-related conditons.' Are you at risk?

What is anxiety?

Anxiety is an unpleasant feeling of fear and apprehension. Normally anxiety can be useful, helping us to avoid dangerous situations, making us alert and giving us the motivation to deal with problems. However, if the feelings become too strong or go on for too long, they can stop us from doing the things we want to, making our lives miserable.

How do you know if you are anxious?

Psychological symptoms:

- Anger
- Fear of madness
- Fear of impending death
- Feelings of being outside yourself
- Feelings of being cut off from reality
- Feeling worried all the time
- Feeling tired
- Feeling irritable
- Irritability
- Poor memory
- Sleeping badly
- Unable to concentrate

Physical symptoms:

- Abdominal discomfort
- Breathing heavily
- Diarrhoea
- Difficulty in swallowing
- Dizziness
- Faintness
- Frequent urination
- Headache
- Indigestion
- Muscle tension and pains
- Racing heart
- Sweating
- Tightness or pain in chest
- Tingling in finger tips

It is quite normal to feel anxious when you are facing something dangerous or difficult, but it is not usual to feel anxious all the time or to feel that anxiety is ruling your life. Extreme anxiety is manifested as phobias, panic attacks or obsessive compulsive disorder.

When anxiety has gone too far . . .

Severe anxiety is similar to a 'false alarm'. Our bodies over-react, and respond with anxiety to something that is not threatening. It can happen if we exaggerate the danger in our

It is quite normal to feel anxious when you are facing something dangerous or difficult, but it is not usual to feel anxious all the time or to feel that anxiety is ruling your life

minds; if we are under stress; or when we start thinking about past difficulties.

Severe anxiety doesn't just fade away; it can be so unpleasant that you begin to find ways of avoiding the situation or event that makes you feel so bad. Every time you succeed in avoiding the event your anxiety level drops and so in the short term you feel better. However long term you can become a recluse avoiding any situation that may evoke anxiety and never knowing whether that danger was all in your mind.

- The above information is from TheSite's website which can be found at www.thesite.org

© *TheSite.org*

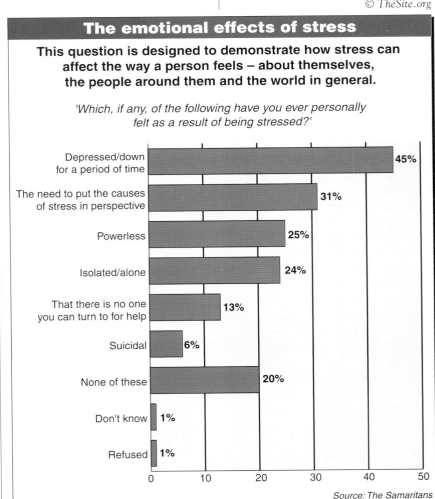

The emotional effects of stress

This question is designed to demonstrate how stress can affect the way a person feels – about themselves, the people around them and the world in general.

'Which, if any, of the following have you ever personally felt as a result of being stressed?'

Response	%
Depressed/down for a period of time	45%
The need to put the causes of stress in perspective	31%
Powerless	25%
Isolated/alone	24%
That there is no one you can turn to for help	13%
Suicidal	6%
None of these	20%
Don't know	1%
Refused	1%

Source: The Samaritans

Issues

www.independence.co.uk

21

The law and stress

Information from UK National Work-Stress Network

There is no discrete law dealing with work-related stress. A number of laws and regulations can be used to deal with the many causes and results of work-related stress.

The Management of Health and Safety at Work Regulations 1999 [including the Approved Code of Practice].

This regulation deals with the requirement on employers to assess the risks to the health and safety of employees and to provide them with comprehensive and relevant information on those risks. It also requires the employer to take into account the individual's capabilities when assessing the risks. Failure to either produce and/or act upon assessments may be evidence of negligence.

The contractual obligation

It is an implied term of every contract of employment that the employer will take care of the health and safety of their employees.

Negligence and liability

Employers must provide a safe place of work, a safe system of work, safe plant and appliances and safe and competent fellow workers. If an employer fails to take reasonable care to protect an employee from a foreseeable injury, by failing to provide any of the above, he or she could be found by the courts to have breached the 'duty of care'. Redress would either be via the Civil or Criminal law.

Disability Discrimination Act 1996

The Disability Discrimination Act came into force in December 1996 and creates new rights for disabled people. It makes it unlawful to discriminate against disabled people in employment, access to goods, services, transport and education. If there is unlawful discrimination, the disabled person can claim compensation from an Industrial Tribunal.

Sex Discrimination Act 1975 and Race Relations Act 1976

Where there is a sexual or racial element to the behaviour causing the stress the employer could be held vicariously liable for the actions of a harassing or bullying employee, even where they were not aware of the behaviour.

Health and Safety at Work etc. Act 1974

Section 2 of the Act places a duty upon all employers to ensure the health (including mental health), safety and welfare of all employees and to create safe and healthy working systems.

Criminal Justice and Public Order Act 1974

This act makes intentional harassment in the workplace a criminal offence punishable by law where the perpetrator in speech or in writing uses abusive or insulting language or behaviour, or disorderly behaviour so that another person feels harassment, alarm or distress.

Employment Protection (Consolidation) Act 1978

An employee may complain to an Industrial Tribunal of constructive dismissal in circumstances where workplace bullying has led to him or her leaving their employment.

Advice and support

Individuals who believe they have been subjected to workplace stress and wish to seek a remedy should consult their trade union representative.

If not a member of a trade union, individuals should seek legal advice. The local Citizens' Advice Bureau can suggest an appropriate local solicitor.

You can also contact someone from the UK National Work-Stress Network who may be able to suggest some additional contacts.

■ More recent legislation has been enacted. For full details of all legislation, visit the UK National Work-Stress Network's website: www.workstress.net

© *UK National Work-Stress Network*

> *A number of laws and regulations can be used to deal with the many causes and results of work-related stress*

'Can't cope culture' bill hits £2bn and rising

The cost of benefits paid to those claiming they have been disabled by stress, depression and anxiety has risen to more than £2 billion a year, prompting a warning by Conservatives of a burgeoning 'can't cope culture'.

Analysis of Government spending on incapacity benefit for various forms of mental disorder suggests claims for stress and depression are soaring, leaving the taxpayer with a ballooning annual bill.

Critics will seize on the figures as further evidence that thousands of otherwise healthy men and women are being kept off the unemployment register by being signed off as unfit to work on mental health grounds.

The statistics are contained in a written parliamentary answer from the work and pensions minister, Maria Eagle, to Paul Goodman, the Tory social security spokesman. He said the figures were shocking.

It is believed to be the first time that an accurate price tag has been put on the trend towards what some experts claim are benefits for vaguely defined disorders that encourage the workshy.

Since Labour came to power in 1997 the cost of benefits for those claiming that they suffer from post-traumatic stress has risen from £48 million a year to £103 million.

For those certified with depression, annual expenditure has risen from £773 million in 1997 to £1,036 million this year.

Phobic anxiety accounts for a further £282 million a year, while all other mental and behavioural disorders absorb £613 million.

More than 700,000 people – a quarter of all claims – receive up to £84 a week in incapacity benefit on the grounds of poor mental health, a 38 per cent increase since 1997. Of those, 232,300 are women, a 60 per cent increase in seven years.

Stress and depression – the two causes showing the sharpest increases

By Benedict Brogan, Political Correspondent

since 1997 – now account for 65 per cent of all mental health cases.

Gordon Brown, the Chancellor, cites the Government's success at driving down unemployment and increasing the number of jobs in the economy as evidence of Labour's economic competence.

Analysis of Government spending on incapacity benefit for various forms of mental disorder suggests claims for stress and depression are soaring

But some experts believe that success is a result of switching a significant number of people claiming the jobseekers' allowance – the main unemployment benefit – to incapacity benefit.

Figures released in May 2004 showed that the number of people of working age who are economically inactive is at record levels – more than 7.8 million, an increase of 250,000 since 1997.

The number of people claiming incapacity benefit has soared under the Tories and Labour, more than trebling to 2.7 million since 1979.

The Government pays out £16 billion a year on incapacity benefit, compared with £4 billion in unemployment benefit.

Mr Goodman said: 'These figures are shocking. They prove that claims for depression, stress and anxiety are out of control and the Government doesn't have a clue how to respond.

'Ministers need to come forward with urgent proposals to show they can get claims under control and reduce the burden on the taxpayer.

'If people are being signed off too easily and are capable of work then it's hidden unemployment.'

He added: 'It's impossible to believe that many of these people are not capable of work.

'There is a danger here of a "can't cope" culture.'

© Telegraph Group Limited, London 2005

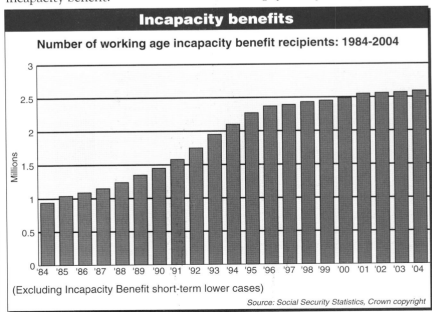

Incapacity benefits

Number of working age incapacity benefit recipients: 1984-2004

(Excluding Incapacity Benefit short-term lower cases)

Source: Social Security Statistics, Crown copyright

Cope with stress at work

Beat the burnout. Tackle pressure before it takes hold . . .

The recent tale of a City trader who lost her bank almost £4m when she went home early one day because of stress shows just how damaging workplace worries can be. And the sales-driven recruitment industry is one sector where stress is rife.

According to the Health & Safety Executive, there is a clear link between stress and ill-health. The HSE's research recently discovered that more than 105m days are lost to stress each year, costing UK employers £1.24bn.

Work-related stress is a serious economic problem. And, as the HSE points out, the law also requires employers to take action on the matter.

Many people thrive under pressure. But problems start when those pressures exceed a person's ability to cope. First of all, we have to ask ourselves what causes stress? It's impossible to specify the external conditions that cause stress as everyone's interpretation of a stressful situation is different.

That said, some situations are more stressful than others, such as perhaps going to the dentist, having surgery, moving job, school or house,

By Neil Shah, Praesto Training & Development

getting married or divorced, or the pressure of meeting targets and deadlines. Furthermore, situations arise on a day-to-day basis that make physical, mental and emotional demands on us.

Stress is the driving force that keeps us on our toes and pushes us to be the best we can. However, that is only valid up to a certain point. Too much stress can drive us into physical, mental and emotional exhaustion.

> *Many people thrive under pressure. But problems start when those pressures exceed a person's ability to cope*

Having too little stress can also be a problem. If we are not stretched or committed, we can become bored, sluggish and lethargic. Therefore it is imperative to strike a balance.

How does stress make us feel? When a stressful situation is interpreted as dangerous or threatening, people experience feelings of tension, apprehension and worry. These feelings may also be accompanied by behavioural and physiological changes, such as trembling, palpitations, dizziness, tremors and so on.

Internal stress-causing factors combine with these external signs. Many kinds of internal conflicts can cause stress; the most common is a feeling of wanting to do something but feeling you shouldn't, or the feeling you should be doing something when you don't really want to.

Stress and anxiety both require energy, and once this energy is used up, the person becomes depressed; there is no energy left to feed the anxieties, so they are never resolved. To avoid this, we must take stock of all aspects of our life and situations. If treated early, the prospects are good. If left, there is a risk that burnout may become a permanent state of affairs.

A useful strategy for dealing with a sense of being overwhelmed by all the things that need attention is prioritising and diarising.

Make a list of all the things you need to do, list them in order of genuine importance, noting what you need to do personally and what can be delegated to others, as well as what needs to be done immediately and in the next week or month.

Viewed this way, your initially overwhelming and unmanageable list – the main source of stress – can become a more realistic and manageable set of tasks. allowing you to sleep a good deal easier at night.

■ From the *Recruiter Magazine*, 12 May 2004.

■ The above information is from the Stress Management Society's website which can be found at www.stress.org.uk

© *The Stress Management Society*

Managing stress in others

Information from the Chartered Management Institute

Stress can be defined as demands on physical, mental and emotional energies. Such demands can be normal or exceptional, and are experienced both at home and at work.

People who consider that stress is both inevitable and helpful are partially correct. Reasonable levels of stress at work are necessary for people to perform well, while low levels of stress can lead people to become demotivated and lethargic. Excessive stress levels, however, are not acceptable, and seem to have a cumulatively harmful effect on people.

J. M. Atkinson defines stress at work as ' . . . an excess of perceived demands over an individual's perceived ability to meet them . . .'. Such high levels of stress, especially if sustained over a long period of time, will:

- seriously undermine performance at individual, team and organisational levels
- damage the health and wellbeing of individual sufferers
- affect relationships both at work and at home
- leave both the organisation and responsible managers open to possible high legal costs, in the long term.

Recent research suggests that excessive stress is an increasing problem for many people in the United Kingdom. In the year 2000, for example, the Health and Safety Executive estimated that 6.5 million working days are lost annually in the UK due to work stress. This represents a cost of between £353 and £381 million to the economy (at 1995/96 prices), and the loss is increasing year on year, with an estimated 500% increase since the 1950s.

There are many factors contributing to experiences of excessive stress in the workplace. These include:

- job insecurity
- organisational culture
- new technology
- unreasonable expectations
- lack of communication and involvement
- organisational changes, such as restructuring, mergers or take-overs.

In order to accommodate such changes, individuals often need to make fundamental shifts in the way they work as their workloads increase, and it becomes more difficult to maintain a healthy balance between their work and their home lives.

Studies suggest that stress is closely related to the degree of control that individuals have over their work. While self-imposed, temporary pressure can be tolerated at a very high level, the threshold for pressure imposed from outside can be low. Previous experiences, perceptions and attitudes will also affect responses to stressful situations.

The experience of stress is linked to a genetically inherited, adrenalin-priming (but now inappropriate) 'flight or fight' response to stressful situations that would have helped us to survive, in a prehistoric context. While we cannot run or fight in response to high stress, we still experience the bodily changes that would enable us to do so, and this has a physical wear-and-tear effect upon us. Symptoms of excessive stress in individuals include:

- headaches

- disturbed sleep
- loss of appetite and indigestion
- irritability and tension
- skin problems
- loss of energy.

Under stress, people become demotivated and forgetful, and are less able to concentrate. If the situation continues, their symptoms may worsen and panic attacks, hyperventilation, tearfulness and depression may develop. In teams or organisations, signs of stress can include:

- lower commitment
- missed deadlines
- reluctance to communicate
- increased conflicts
- absenteeism.

As a manager you are responsible for monitoring your own stress levels and those of the people who work for you. You should be aware of how your style of management and personal behaviour patterns could cause stress to others, or give them a poor example of stress management. Your role is central in acting as a buffer for your team, giving them support, and helping them to manage and cope with work and other life pressures. For this, it is essential to learn how to:

- recognise stress warning signs in individuals, teams and organisations
- maintain perspective and balance
- take steps to reduce the stress.

Reference
1. *Coping with stress at work: how to stop worrying and start succeeding*, J.M. Atkinson, Wellingborough: Thorsons, 1988.

- Reproduced by kind permission of the the Chartered Management Institute, the leading organisation for managers in the UK. The guidelines of stress management, along with many other 'spotlights on management topics', can be found at www.managers.org.uk/mic

© *Chartered Management Institute*

Let's stop stressing about stress

By Sarfraz Manzoor

I have been stressing out all week about what to write today. The pressures of the impending deadline inducing the all-too-familiar sensations of fear, panic and helplessness. In fact, my own stress levels were only alleviated when I read that today is National Stress Awareness Day.

The truth is that I would not have it any other way; if it were not for stress I doubt whether I would get anything done. The Health and Safety Executive, however, defines stress as 'the adverse reaction people have to excessive pressure or other types of demand placed on them'. This sounds fair enough, except that assessing what might be considered 'excessive pressure' is bound to be problematic and, let's be honest, open to abuse. An estimated 13.5 million days are lost each year due to self-reported work-related stress, depression or anxiety, costing the economy £7bn a year in sick pay, lost productivity and health costs. The stress industry is clearly big business but rather than challenging complaints about stress in the workplace the government – whose own civil servants take an average two weeks' sick leave a year – has laid out a new code for reducing stress; one that will put employers at risk of legal action if they ignore it.

So, why are we all so stressed? There are, it seems to me, two possible explanations. The first is that the demands of modern living and the pressures of today's work culture are greater than at any time in history; the second is that we have all become a nation of wimps. Those who buy into the first explanation claim that Britain has the longest working hours in Europe – that the impact of management-efficiency drives has left employees drowning in their work. That may all be true, but I find it hard to believe that today's office employees are really the most overworked group in history.

As a young boy I remember my father coming home after having worked a 12-hour shift at the Vauxhall car plant. Each night he would get home, eat and then work till the small hours of the morning helping my mother as she made dresses on her sewing machine. Four hours of sleep later, he would be up again for work. That was his life, seven days a week, yet I don't once recall him complaining about suffering from stress or threatening to sue General Motors for the 'excessive pressure' they were putting him under. He understood that our jobs are called work for a reason: that is meant to be what they are. There is a word for doing things that is pleasurable, and that is a hobby.

> **An estimated 13.5 million days are lost each year due to self-reported work-related stress, depression or anxiety, costing the economy £7bn a year in sick pay, lost productivity and health costs**

There are, of course, jobs that I would agree are unreasonably stressful – cockle-picking for example – and many others that are brutalising in their monotony. In most cases, however, what we now refer to as stress would once have been called life. As our jobs have become less physically dangerous there has been a corresponding rush to claim that our office-based lives are liable to lead to psychological problems. Opportunist lawyers and trade unions have been quick to claim stress as a medical ailment and yet it seems to me that if stress is a disease, it is a disease of affluence. It is a byproduct of too many choices and unrealistic expectations about work.

With our long working hours, with more and more people living alone, our jobs define who we are to a greater degree than ever before. Because they mean so much more they need to be more fulfilling; it is not enough that they pay the mortgage. If they are not fulfilling – if they are challenging or frustrating – it is now not only acceptable but almost required that you complain and bemoan how work is not making you feel 'included' or 'in control'. That, I think, might be the reason why it is usually white-collar workers who complain loudest about work stress: it is not that blue-collar workers are blissfully relaxed, they just have different expectations about their jobs.

There is a depressing defeatism in the attitude that the best response to challenges at work is to call them stress and chuck a sickie. It is an attitude that assumes that we need professional help to cope with stress; when stress is simply an umbrella term that could describe all manner of normal emotions. It is hard not to be suspicious that many of the days taken off and the compensation claimed in the name of stress in truth have their roots in frustration, boredom and insecurity. Not to mention incompetence.

These days, my personal experience of stress is limited to the demands of the deadline. But perhaps because I remember when all I wanted was the stress of being in employment, and perhaps because I was raised by parents who did not assume my wellbeing was anyone else's responsibility, I find the current obsession with work pressures alien and offensive. We need to chill out about stress.

A ten-step guide to coping with stress

Information from the Stress Management Society

1) Avoid nicotine, alcohol and caffeine.
They are all stimulants, so therefore they cannot calm you down. If you're stressed, steer clear of them and keep yourself well-hydrated by drinking water instead.

2) Work off stress with physical activity.
Pressure or anger releases adrenalin in the body. Exercise helps to reduce it, and produces 'good mood' substances in the brain. So go for a brisk walk around the block when you feel tense, and try some regular exercise after work.

3) Relax with a stress reduction technique every day.
Try self-hypnosis – it's very easy and can even be done at your desk. We can recommend courses in self-hypnosis and will soon be bringing out a CD that will teach you the secrets of this technique. Email us for details on info@stress.org.uk. Or think up a self-affirming mantra to repeat to yourself (e.g. 'I deserve calm in my life', or 'I have a choice in every situation'). Repeat it to yourself whenever you feel tense.

4) Get enough sleep.
Sleep is essential for the body to function properly. Sleeping pills are not necessary if you change your lifestyle. If you've habitually skimped on sleep, you probably won't even remember how it feels to wake up fully rested. Give it a go for a week, and see if there's a difference in how you perform during the day.

5) If you're ill, rest.
Don't just carry on regardless. Working will tire the body and prolong the illness. So recognise that you have limits and don't carry on as if you were firing on all cylinders.

6) Agree with somebody; once in a while!
Life shouldn't be a constant battleground. So even if you disagree with someone, avoid conflict by just agreeing or keeping quiet. After all, they have a right to their opinion, just as you do.

7) Learn to accept what you cannot change.
A well-known prayer asks for the serenity 'to accept the things I cannot change, the courage to change the things I can, and the wisdom to know the difference'. This philosophy will help you avoid unhappiness, cynicism and bitterness.

8) Listen to your body.
When you are tired, hungry or thirsty, do something about it. Also recognise stress and anger in your day and counter it immediately with a brisk walk, ten minutes in deep relaxation or whatever works for you. Order a batch of our 'stress spots' to put around the house or office so you can test your stress levels whenever you like.

9) Learn how to say 'no'.
Simple, but effective. Where a 'no' is the appropriate response, say it without guilt.

10) Manage your time.
Take one thing at a time. Don't overdo things. Create time buffers to deal with unexpected emergencies. And, recognise that your day-to-day problems and responsibilities are the things that cause stress in your life. Tackle them with a system that works for you. A simple method is to:

- List the things that you need to do.
- Put them in order of importance.
- Decide what you need to do yourself, and what can be delegated.
- Decide which needs doing today, next week or next month.
- Decide what doesn't need doing after all, and drop it from the list.

Your mountain of tasks is now in some sort of order. This should help. The list used to control you. Now you control it. And you've lost the stress that it caused you.

- The above information is from the Stress Management Society's website which can be found at www.stress.org.uk

Managing stress

Information from MIND

**For better
mental health**

This information is aimed at anyone who wants to know how to cut down their stress levels. It explains when and how stress can be bad for you, and describes the signs to watch out for. It also provides helpful strategies for dealing with stress.

'The more I did, the more I seemed to have to do. I felt as if I was on the verge of flu, but it never seemed either to turn into full-blown illness, or to go away. Eventually, after a good few weeks, I went to the doctor, and she said what I needed was a holiday, and she wished she could give it to me on prescription.'

'I was so worried about the money, but there was nothing I could do. I felt I couldn't worry my wife about it, so I kept quiet about it. Eventually, she wheedled it out of me. It was such a relief. Telling her about it made me realise I'd got the whole thing out of proportion.'

'I was on a short fuse with everything and everyone, and it was a sort of vicious circle, because then the whole family began to snap at each other. I couldn't understand what was wrong. I just wanted to shut myself away. But, then, when I was on my own, I felt as if everyone else was having a better time without me. I'd wake up in the middle of the night and not get back to sleep, and I was getting more and more tired. Things didn't start getting better until I realised that I had to change the way I was organising my life, and let other people take on some of the strain.'

When and why is stress harmful?

Stress is something we all encounter. Life changes, such as moving house, getting married or coping with a bereavement, can all cause it, while negative social conditions, such as unemployment, poor housing, noisy neighbours, relationship problems and difficulties at work, can also contribute. However, stress also has a positive side. A certain level of stress may be necessary and enjoyable in order to spark us into action.

Stress means different things to different people. A situation that is intolerable to one person may be stimulating to another. What you feel is determined not just by events and changes in the outside world, but how you perceive and respond to them. The important point is that you can learn to recognise your own responses to stress and, if necessary, develop skills to deal with it.

In the animal world, the response to danger is to run away or to turn and fight. People respond to emotional stress as if it were a physical threat; rapid changes in the muscles and organs of the body are involved. Your muscles tense, ready for action and your heart beats faster to carry blood to where it's most needed – the muscles and the brain. You breathe faster, sweat more and your mouth becomes dry. These physical reactions are due to hormones that the body produces, including one called adrenalin.

This automatic reaction to a threatening situation is known as the 'fight or flight' reaction. It equips us to fight or escape from an enemy. You may merely be having an argument with a colleague, but your body may react as though you were gripped in a life-or-death struggle with a lion. Unfortunately, many people turn to cigarettes, alcohol or tranquillisers as a way of coping with stress. These may seem to help in the short term, but in the longer term, may further undermine your well-being.

How can I tell if I'm under too much stress?

As stress begins to take its toll physically, emotionally and on your behaviour, a variety of symptoms can result. Check off the symptoms you recognise in the following lists. If you identify a large number of signs in yourself, don't panic! You're among those who can benefit from applying the principles and techniques outlined in this information.

How your body may react
- breathlessness
- feeling sick or dizzy
- headaches
- constant tiredness
- fainting spells
- restlessness
- chest pains
- sleeping problems
- tendency to sweat
- constipation or diarrhoea
- nervous twitches
- craving for food
- cramps or muscle spasms
- indigestion or heartburn
- pins and needles
- lack of appetite
- high blood pressure
- sexual difficulties

How you may feel
- aggressive
- a loss of interest in others
- irritable
- taking no interest in life
- depressed
- neglect ded
- bad or ugly

- that there's no one to confide in
- fearing diseases
- fearing failure
- a loss of sense of humour
- dreading the future

How you may behave
- have difficulty making decisions
- avoiding difficult situations
- have difficulty concentrating
- frequently crying
- denying there's a problem
- biting your nails
- unable to show true feelings

In ticking off your own reactions, you can get an idea of your characteristic responses to stress.

What's the best way to handle pressure?

Remember that a little stress is good for the body and alerts the mind. However, the methods of coping with stress described in this article should enable you to deal more effectively with it.

Manage your time
Although we often plan for months ahead, it's also important to plan our days. Making time for leisure, exercise and holidays is just as essential as spending time on business or home worries.

- Everybody has a time when they feel at their best. Identify your best time (you may be a morning person or a night owl) and use it to carry out important tasks that need the most energy and concentration.
- Make a list of things you have to do on any given day. These are your priorities; everything else can be left until later. Arrange these priorities in order of importance, and stick to that order.
- Try to take tasks one at a time, until each is finished. If you try to do too many at once, you're more likely to end up muddled and accomplishing less.
- Variety is a good idea. If you can, vary your tasks in a day; dull jobs with interesting tasks, tiring jobs with easier ones.

Act positively
- Once you've finished a task, take a few moments to pause and relax.

Make a list of things you have to do on any given day. These are your priorities; everything else can be left until later

Remember to use your break wisely: do you really need that cigarette or cup of coffee? Why not eat an apple or try some deep breathing instead?

- In the face of unrealistic demands and expectations coming from other people, be prepared to say no. Practise being straightforward and assertive in communicating with others.
- At the end of each day, sit back and reflect on what you've done and what you've achieved, rather than spending time worrying about what still needs to be done.
- Try to make time to switch off from your tasks at home or at work. Use your free time to relax and unwind.
- A change of scene can help. Try to get away every so often, even if only for a couple of days.
- Develop an absorbing hobby or interest, one that is far removed from everyday stresses and strains; you'll be glad you did.

How can I overcome the ill effects of stress?
Sleep problems
Sleep problems, such as insomnia, are a common sign of stress. A recent survey showed that one in five people has them. Worries about personal problems, family, or work may make it increasingly difficult to fall asleep, and sleep may be disturbed by vivid, bad dreams. There are several simple measures worth trying if you want to establish a better sleeping pattern.

- Pay attention to your surroundings. If you are troubled by noise, use earplugs; if light from the street disturbs you, use thick, lined curtains or blinds.
- It makes sense to wake up at the same time each morning and go to bed at about the same time every night. Usually, if people get up regularly at the same hour, they will tend to become sleepy

---

by a certain hour in the evening.
- It can be helpful to follow a night-time routine in order to wind down before bedtime. You could try going for a walk, listening to the radio or watching a relaxing TV programme, reading an undemanding magazine, taking a warm bath or having a hot drink (but avoid stimulants, such as tea and coffee, and heavy meals, late at night). Relaxation and deep breathing exercises can also help you switch off and prepare for sleep.

Many middle-aged and older people feel that they sleep less well than they would like, but people do tend to sleep less soundly as they get older. Physical discomfort or pain will certainly affect sleep, but it's worth noting that drugs prescribed for an illness may also cause insomnia.

Underlying emotional problems can make people much more vulnerable to stress. Depression may make it difficult for you to get to sleep, or you may find you wake very early feeling particularly depressed and anxious. Consider contacting your GP to discuss your sleep problem. Alternatively, if you wish to explore any underlying reasons, you could consider counselling.

The holistic approach to health-care emphasises the need to look at the whole person and not just their problems, and this can also be very helpful for stress-related symptoms. Many practitioners of alternative and complementary medicine take a holistic approach. Meditation, massage and autogenics can all help relieve stress disorders and promote relaxation.

How can I help myself to relax?
Relaxation is the natural answer to stress. Each and every one of us should make time in the day to relax, whether we feel under stress, or not. The following techniques can help.

Deep breathing
The way you breathe can have a dramatic effect on your sense of wellbeing. Many people breathe poorly, without even realising it. This is especially true of people under stress. To improve the way you breathe, try this simple exercise for

just five minutes a day. It can help relieve tension, anxiety, dizziness, pins and needles, cramps and chest pains.

Don't be concerned if these breathing exercises aren't for you. Not everyone feels comfortable focusing on their breathing, and if this is the case, there's no need to pursue it.

- Sit down, or lie down on your back. Make sure you are comfortable, and loosen any tight clothing.
- Become aware of your breathing, its rhythm, depth or shallowness, and its speed.
- Put one hand on your upper chest and one just below your ribs on your abdomen.
- Slowly let out your breath.
- Gently breathe in, so that you feel your abdomen rise slowly under your hand.
- Breathe out again, feeling your abdomen fall, and make sure you exhale a little longer than you inhaled.
- Pause for a few moments and then repeat the process again.

If you find that only the hand on your abdomen moves, then you are breathing correctly; the abdomen is moving as your diaphragm rises and falls rhythmically. There should be little or no movement in your upper chest; your hand should stay still.

Simple relaxation

Try this every now and again, especially when you feel under pressure. It should take you no more than five to ten minutes.

- Have a stretch. Then let your shoulders and arms relax into a comfortable position. Shrugging, wriggling and shaking all help your muscles to stop tensing and to relax.
- Ease off the tension in your feet, ankles, calves, knees, thighs, chest, arms and neck.
- If you are sitting in a chair, or on the floor, allow yourself to feel as if the chair or the floor is supporting your whole weight; feel yourself letting go.
- Try to be peaceful; loosen your jaw and face. A bland expression will help your face muscles to relax.

- Follow the breathing technique just described.
- Close your eyes and imagine a peaceful scene, such as an exotic desert island, the shady depths of a forest, or sunlight glistening on a lake.
- Choose your own special place, whatever seems most restful to you. Then for a few moments, imagine that you are really there.

What else can I do to reduce my stress levels?

Exercise

Physical activity is an important means of reducing stress levels and preventing some of its damaging effects on the body. Exercise uses up the adrenalin and other hormones that the body produces under stress, and relaxes the muscles. It will help to strengthen the heart and improve blood circulation, too.

Research suggests that physical activity can lead to a change in body chemistry that can affect the way people feel, as well as their physical condition. And that's not all. Exercise can also help to raise self-esteem and reduce anxiety and depression.

You don't necessarily have to take up a competitive or vigorous new sport. Remember that you can benefit simply by becoming more active, as part of your daily routine. So, walk to the shops, don't drive, climb the stairs, don't use the lift, cultivate your garden, don't just sit there!

Healthy eating

When things get too hectic or difficult, and you feel under stress, it's often easy to forget about what you eat; it just doesn't seem important, or there isn't time. But what we eat, and when we eat, can make a big difference. It's important to make time for regular food or snacks and not to miss out on meals, such as breakfast. Try not to rush; take time to enjoy what you're eating.

Choose a good variety of foods, making sure you have a balance of protein (from meat, fish, nuts or cheese), starch (from bread, potatoes, pasta and rice) and fibre (cereal and wholemeal bread). Eat plenty of fresh fruit and vegetables (a minimum of five portions a day). Finally, cut down on saturated fat (from dairy products), sugary foods and salt.

Having fun

Making time for regular leisure activities can help you release the tension that stress can cause, and to take your mind off the worries of the day. Whether you unwind by soaking in a hot bath, browsing through your favourite books, listening to music, gardening or taking photographs, the important point is to enjoy the activity as an end in itself, purely for the pleasure of the moment.

- The above information is from the *Mind guide to managing stress*.

Stress and your heart

Information from the British Heart Foundation

Coping with stress

You may find that making changes to your lifestyle helps to reduce the effects of stress on your body.

Action points

- take more exercise
- eat well, and drink plenty of water
- cut down on drinking alcohol, smoking and drugs
- make more time for rest and relaxation
- seek help or information – for example about time management, stress management, or assertiveness training
- get support. Talk to friends, workmates or family. Or find out about joining a support group or having counselling
- learn to say 'No' when you feel over-burdened.

Changing your lifestyle in this way can make you feel physically fitter and better able to cope with some of the demands on you – and more able to cope with stressful situations. However you experience stress, coping well with stressful situations can help you feel in control of life and good about yourself.

A healthy lifestyle

A balanced diet and 30 minutes of moderate intensity activity on at least 5 days a week will help you to cope with stress. It will also give you:

- more energy and stamina
- more confidence and a positive self-image
- a stronger, toned body
- a lower risk of coronary heart disease, diabetes, stroke and cancer.

Stress can make you feel like you don't want to do things, but try to make the effort. Even a brisk half-hour walk every day can make a difference to how you feel, look and cope with life.

Eat well, and drink plenty of water. People under stress often feel the need for high-calorie snacks and sweets. Coupled with a lack of activity, this can lead to weight gain and tiredness. Instead, try the following:

- eat regular meals
- have at least 5 portions of fruit and vegetables a day
- make sure that at least one-third of your food comes from bread, pasta, beans, rice, potatoes or pulses
- cut down on salt and sugar
- have less coffee, tea and other drinks with caffeine; and drink plenty of water.

Case study

Soon after Karen started a new job, her father died from a heart attack. She already had these two big, life-changing events to cope with, and then fell down the stairs and fractured her ankle, ending up with her leg in plaster for eight weeks. When Karen returned to work she found she was enjoying being back and that she was happier, but she was still under a lot of stress which was affecting her physically. She had painful muscular tension in her neck, shoulders and back.

Karen did two things to help reduce her stress levels. First, she contacted her Human Resources Department to ask for a work station assessment to see if anything could be done to help relieve her physical symptoms. They gave her advice on how to change her working environment. Secondly, she took up exercise. Karen found that swimming and pilates helped relieve her stress and that they lifted her mood when she was feeling stressed or 'down'. Exercise made Karen feel really positive and energetic. She also tries to book a holiday or a short break

away so that she has something to look forward to during the year.

Don't smoke!

Smoking is not a good short-term prop for stressful situations. If you have already tried to quit smoking and started again, ask your doctor or pharmacist about the stop smoking aids now available. Nicotine replacement products help to wean you off nicotine by replacing the very high concentrations of nicotine you get from smoking by delivering lower doses more slowly. If you smoke mainly in response to stress, the gum, lozenges, microtabs, nasal spray or inhalator might be a good choice for you. Or ask your doctor about bupropion – a non-nicotine treatment, available on NHS prescrip-tion. Bupropion works in the brain to help break the addiction to nicotine. Both nicotine replacement products and bupropion can reduce the cravings for cigarettes and the withdrawal symptoms associated with quitting.

Keep your alcohol intake within the healthy limits

- no more than 21 units a week for men
- no more than 14 units a week for women
- have at least two alcohol-free days each week

All the following drinks contain about 1 unit of alcohol:

- 1 pint of ordinary strength beer, lager or cider
- 1 small glass of wine
- 1 single pub measure of spirits
- 1 small glass of sherry
- 1 single measure of an apéritif.

Make more time for rest and relaxation We all need relaxation and we all choose to do different things. Each day should include a relaxing activity – for example listening to music, walking the dog or spending time with friends. Make a list of things that help you to relax, and schedule one in every day. For some people relaxation classes can be helpful.

Time management

If you need help with managing your time, or you find that you never get done all the things you need to do, you may find a book or a course on time management helpful.

Stress management

Advice on stress management may involve relaxation training, or learning how to handle different sources of stress and to manage attitudes and behaviours that increase stress. For details of local courses, contact the International Stress Management Association.

Assertiveness training

If you find that you have too much to do because you can't say 'No', you may benefit from assertiveness training.

Case study

Carolyn has two small children and finds it hard to 'juggle' her time between work and home. She is finding things stressful at work. She finds it helps to take a step back and get things into perspective by thinking about the things outside work that matter to her, and by looking forward to activities that she has planned for the weekend. She also finds it helpful to plan something that is easily achievable and do some small, easy tasks that she can get out of the way. Carolyn has also found self-help books on managing her time useful.

Case study

Nick has a job that involves regularly driving to and from different parts of the country. He realised that he was finding this very stressful as he often got caught in traffic and arrived late. This meant that he was arriving in a bad mood. He decided to take action by writing out a route plan before setting out on each trip, giving himself an extra half-hour each time to allow for traffic, and having contact phone numbers to hand to call if he is running late. He also keeps some music CDs to help him relax if he gets stuck in traffic. He has learned to practise some deep breathing exercises to reduce tension, and he reminds himself that nobody will suffer as a consequence of him being late. Arriving on time is not a 'life or death' situation.

The stress chain

This shows you just one example of a strategy for coping with stress.

Harmful stress	What you can do
Be aware of it	■ keep a stress diary ■ make a 'hassle list' – a list of things that cause you stress ■ set aside some time to yourself
Reduce the chance of it happening again	■ manage your time
Change how you see it or feel about it	■ get the balance right ■ take a positive approach
Change how you react to it	■ communicate with your partner and with others ■ be assertive about your needs too ■ use humour ■ accept what you can't change
Reduce its effects on your body	■ physical activity ■ massage ■ relaxation

Source: British Heart Foundation

Case study

Shahnaz has recently been under a lot of stress, after separating from her husband and moving into a new home. She has found that talking to someone about her situation has really helped, and has taken comfort in her friends' advice and support. Talking about her problems has helped her to calm down and carry on. Knowing that other people have managed to get through stressful situations helps.

Case study

Milo found that he was feeling tired all the time and had difficulty sleeping. He had visited his GP who ruled out any other reason for his tiredness and insomnia. His GP asked him to consider making changes to his lifestyle. Milo decided that he was going to make an effort to leave work on time at least twice a week and to use the extra time to play tennis with his neighbour. He looked at his diet and realised that he was often skipping meals or eating high-fat, convenience foods. He decided to make an effort to have lunch each day, even when he was really busy, and to eat more fruit and vegetables. After making these changes, Milo found that that he had more energy and felt more positive and better able to cope with stressful situations.

Support from friends

Sharing problems with friends and family can help you to cope with difficult situations. If you are feeling isolated, you may want to widen your circle of friends by joining an evening class, working with a voluntary organisation, or taking up a new hobby.

Support from a counsellor

Some people find it helps to talk to a counsellor. Counselling is never an admission of weakness – it is about making a positive choice to look after yourself. If you don't think that counselling is right for you, then think about other sources of support that could be helpful.

A support group

If you find yourself in a particular situation – for example if you are recently divorced, or if a relative has been diagnosed with a serious health problem – there may be a specific local support group that you can join. A support group gives you the chance to talk to other people who are going through a similar experience. You can share your feelings and coping strategies with each other.

■ The above information is an excerpt from *Stress and your heart*, a booklet produced by the British Heart Foundation: www.bhf.org.uk

© *British Heart Foundation*

Stress and how to cope with it

Information from the Mental Health Foundation

What is stress?

Stress can be defined as the way you feel when you're under abnormal pressure. For example, if you are speaking in public for the first time, if you are rushing to catch the last train home, or if you are made redundant.

All sorts of situations can cause stress. The most common, however, involve work, money matters and relationships with partners, children or other family members. Stress may be caused either by major upheavals and life events such as divorce, unemployment, moving house and bereavement, or by a series of minor irritations such as feeling under-valued at work or dealing with difficult children. Sometimes there are no obvious causes.

Stressful events that are outside the range of normal human ex-perience, for example being abused or tortured, may lead to post-traumatic stress disorder (PTSD).

Some stress can be positive and research has suggested that a moder-ate level of stress makes us perform better. It also makes us more alert and can help us in challenging situations such as job interviews or public speaking. Stressful situations can also be exhilarating and some people actually thrive on the excitement that comes with danger-ous sports or other 'high-risk' activities.

But stress is only healthy as a short-lived response. Excessive or prolonged stress can lead to illness and physical and emotional exhaus-tion. Taken to extremes, stress can be a killer.

What are the symptoms of stress?

Physical changes

When you are stressed, your body produces more of the so-called 'fight or flight' chemicals which prepare your body for an emergency. Adren-alin and noradrenalin raise your blood pressure, increase the rate at which your heart beats and increase the rate at which you perspire. They can also reduce blood flow to your skin and reduce your stomach activity. Cortisol releases fat and sugar into your system (but also reduces the efficiency of your immune system). All of these changes make it easier for you to fight or run away.

Unfortunately these changes are less helpful if you are stuck in a busy office or on an overcrowded train. You can't fight and you can't run

away. Because of this, you can't use the chemicals your own body has produced to protect you. Over time these chemicals and the changes they produce can seriously damage your health.

For example, you may start to experience headaches, nausea and indigestion. You may breathe more quickly, perspire more, have palpitations or suffer from various aches and pains. Longer term you may be putting yourself at risk from heart attacks and stokes.

Emotional changes

When you are stressed you may experience many different feelings, including anxiety, fear, anger, frustration and depression. These feelings can feed on each other and can themselves produce physical symptoms – making you feel even worse. Extreme anxiety can cause giddiness, heart palpitations, head-aches or stomach disorders. Many of these symptoms may make you feel so unwell that you then worry that you have some serious physical conditions such as heart disease or cancer – making you even more stressed.

Behavioural changes

When you are stressed you may behave differently. For example, you may become withdrawn, indecisive or inflexible. You may not be able to sleep properly. You may be irritable or tearful all the time. There may be a change in your sexual habits, and even if you were previously mild-mannered you may suddenly become verbally or physically aggressive.

Who is affected by stress?

All of us can probably recognise at least some of the feelings described above, and may have felt stressed or anxious at some time or other.

Research has shown that around 12 million adults see their GPs with mental health problems each year.

Most of these suffer from anxiety and depression, much of it stress related. It's estimated that about 45 million working days are lost each year through anxiety and stress-related conditions – costing industry more than £3000 million.

Some people seem to be more affected by stress than others. For some people, just getting out of the door on time each morning can be a very stressful experience. Others are more relaxed and easy going and seem to cope better with pressure. If you think you are prone to stress there are various things you can do to help yourself.

How can you help yourself?

- An important step in tackling stress is to realise that it is causing you a problem. You need to make the connection between feeling tired or ill with the pressures you are faced with. Do not ignore physical warnings such as tense muscles, over-tiredness, headaches or migraines.
- If you find yourself becoming angry or upset you may find it helpful to take time out, even if it's only for five minutes. Get yourself a drink of water or take a walk around the block until you feel calmer.
- If you notice you are becoming stressed, try to relax your muscles and calm yourself down by slow, deep breathing. Start by taking a deep breath, hold this for a count of three and then slowly breathe out. Continue this slow breathing until you feel more relaxed and then continue with what you were doing.
- Once you have recognised you are suffering from stress, try to identify the underlying causes. Sort the possible reasons for your stress into those with a practical solution, those that will get better anyway, given time, and those you can't do anything about. Try to let go of those in the second and third groups – there is no point in worrying about things you can't change or things that will sort themselves out.
- Some problems may be more complicated and need to be dealt with head-on. If you are going

through a bad patch in your marriage, for instance, you have to begin to talk things through. This might be difficult to do unaided, so you may need to call on outside help from an organisation like Relate which has trained counsellors.
- Once you've started to deal with the immediate causes of stress, try to review your lifestyle. Are you taking on too much? Are there things you are doing which could be handed over to someone else? Can you do things in a more leisurely way? You may need to prioritise things you are trying to achieve and reorganise your life so that you are not trying to do everything at once.
- You can help protect yourself from stress in a number of ways. For example a healthy diet will help prevent you becoming overweight and will reduce the risks of other diet-related diseases.
- If possible, try to keep smoking and drinking to a minimum. They may seem to reduce tension, but in fact they can make problems worse. They can put you at more risk of physical consequences of stress because of the damage done to the body. You may also find it helpful to reduce the amount of coffee you are drinking as the effects of caffeine on the body can be very similar to the effects of stress and anxiety.
- Physical exercise can be very effective in relieving stress. If you are feeling angry, for example, it can be really helpful to play a game of bitter squash in which you take out your anger on the ball (but not on the player). Even moderate physical exercise, like walking to the shops, can help.

- Take time to relax. Saying 'I just can't take the time off' is no use if you are forced to take time off later through ill health. Striking a balance between responsibility to others and responsibility to yourself is vital in reducing stress levels. Relaxation classes can help you learn how to control muscular tension and breathe correctly. Alternatively you could try to spend more time on leisure activities such as sports, hobbies or evening classes.
- Sleeping problems are common when you're suffering from stress, but try to ensure you get enough rest. Try not to take sleeping pills for longer than a night or two.
- One of the best antidotes for stress is enjoying yourself so try to bring some fun into your life by giving yourself treats and rewards for positive actions, attitudes and thoughts. Even simple pleasures like a relaxing bath, a pleasant walk, or an interesting book can all help you deal with stress.
- Try to keep things in proportion and don't be too hard on yourself. After all, we all have bad days.

Seeking help

Do not be afraid to seek professional help if you feel that you are no longer able to manage things on your own. Many people feel reluctant to seek help as they feel that it is an admission of failure. This is not the case and it is important to get help as soon as possible so you can begin to get better.

The first person to approach is your family doctor. He or she should be able to advise about treatment and may refer you to another local professional such as a counsellor. Treatment can involve talking your problems through with someone trained to deal with stress conditions and may also mean the use of medication for a short period. There are also a number of voluntary organisations which can help you to tackle the causes of stress and advise you about ways to get better.

- The above information is from the Mental Health Foundation's website which can be found at www.mentalhealth.org.uk
© *Mental Health Foundation*

'Life should be fun!'

Information from International Stress Management Association (UK)

How many times have you said that to yourself? Perhaps as you have crawled to work in all that traffic, stared at that unexpected bill or worried that you just can't cope any longer at work.

For life to be enjoyable we all need challenges that we feel we can cope with. Sadly we are all, at times, faced with challenges that we feel we cannot cope with and it is then that we may experience stress.

Showing signs of stress does not mean you are a weak individual who cannot cope! It means you are human like everyone else! People react differently to the situations they have to face because they are all unique individuals. Some may be very passive personalities whilst others may be very competitive. Their life experiences will vary enormously as will their overall conditioning. Their state of health will also vary – it is far more difficult coping with the pressures of everyday life when one is feeling unwell.

Life today is very different to that of only a few years ago. It is very time pressured and competitive. Technology is changing daily. Sadly marriage/partnership breakdowns are becoming very common and long-term job security seems, for many, to be something of the past. It is hardly surprising that at times people feel they just cannot cope.

Some of the most common signs of stress are:
- Mood swings
- Anxiety
- Skin problems
- Tiredness
- Muscle tension
- Poor concentration
- Changes in sleep patterns
- Changes in eating patterns
- Low self-esteem
- Poor memory

Drowning your frustration in alcohol, eating junk foods, self-medicating with drugs such as nicotine – this is not the answer.

It is very important to take positive action when faced with stress as, if experienced over a period of time, it can seriously impair your mental and physical health

The following proven coping strategies can really start to help you reduce the effects of any stress in your life.
- Be aware of your own warning signs – maybe this could be a sudden feeling of anxiety, extreme tiredness, feeling very tearful, catching every cough and cold – feeling run down.
- Review what is really causing stress for you. You could be surprised! Think about what action you could perhaps take to change things. How much of your stress is caused by you? Are your expectations of yourself and others realistic for example?
- At times of stress we often fall into the trap of not eating properly, smoking more or turning to alcohol as a supposedly helpful crutch. (That possible hangover, let alone 'guilt trip' the next day could just add to your problems!) Instead:
- Try and eat a balanced diet.
- Eat complex carbohydrates (such as wholemeal bread, jacket potatoes etc.) rather than refined (that packet of sugary biscuits!).
- This can really help with those mood swings.
- Eat plenty of fresh fruit and vegetables and keep sugar and salt intake to a minimum. This can help to support your immune system in its fight against colds and flu – ailments you so often get when run down.
- Drink plenty of water, it will help you rehydrate your body, and only drink alcohol in moderation.
- Try and keep caffeine consumption to the minimum.
- Try not to turn to nicotine or any other self-prescribed drugs.

- Do not feel guilty about including a period of relaxation every day. We all need to turn off from time to time. Do something you enjoy and that fits into your life. This could, for example, be reading, listening to music, doing yoga or meditating, enjoying a warm bath with perhaps some aromatherapy oils added to it. It does not have to take long – or be considered a luxury or time wasting. It is a vital part of life.
- Make sure exercise is part of life. Exercise which is suitable for you. If you have any doubts as to the correct sort for you ask your doctor.
- Do you often find yourself saying 'yes' when in fact you mean 'no'? Are you always late for things? Do you get frustrated knowing you could have done a better job if you had organised your time

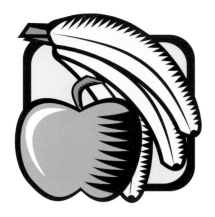

better? Learn how to be more assertive and manage your time properly. Many of us waste so much time – often making excuses for things we have not done! There are some excellent courses available as well as books on both these subjects.
- Consider attending a stress management training course. You

do not have to be stressed to attend one of these. It is far better to know fully what to do prior to experiencing stress than during! We would be happy to supply information about some of the courses that are available.
- There are times when we all need the help and confidential support of other people. Don't be afraid to ask for help if you need it. It can be so helpful. If you wish to be put in contact with a local stress counsellor/therapist we can put you in contact with the one nearest to you.

■ The above information is from the International Stress Management Association UK's website which can be found at www.isma.org.uk
© *International Stress Management Association (UK)*

Top 10 tips for busting stress

What are the secrets of dealing with stress – and of relieving it? Two experts on stress – Dr Roger Henderson, GP and medical columnist; and agony aunt Ingrid Millar – each suggest five stressbusting techniques to get you started . . .

First, Dr Roger Henderson with some top tips on beating stress.

1. Keep a diary
Keep a list – for at least a fortnight – of events, times, places and people that seem to make you feel more stressed. You will probably be surprised to find that a pattern soon emerges; and this may be linked to time pressure, personality clashes, inappropriate demands or simply trying to do too many things at once. Once you have identified your pressure points you can move on to the following solutions . . .

2. Talk
Talk through your diary with a good friend or your partner – even the act of discussing things often makes you feel better. Ask for impartial

advice as to how to ease the problems that you have discovered, or choose the sort of stressful situations that you have identified in which to use the following relaxation techniques.

3. Learn how to relax
- Practise deep-breathing techniques such as slowly inhaling while counting to five; hold your breath for five seconds then breathe out slowly. Repeat this 10 times when feeling stressed, concentrating on nothing but your breathing.
- Stretch the muscles of your neck and shoulders by keeping your shoulders level and trying to touch each shoulder with your ear. Look right up at the ceiling, down at the floor and then

rotate each shoulder in a wide circle. Repeat five times. Open and close your jaw widely after each time since stress often causes tenseness in the jaw area.
- Take time out. For five minutes every hour, try to 'shut down' and think of nothing but your perfect situation. This could be a dream holiday, ideal partner or simply thinking about doing nothing at all. You will be surprised at how effectively this can lower stress levels.

4. Exercise regularly
You do not have to be a gym freak to get the stress-beating benefits of exercise. Even 20 minutes of brisk walking three times a week will help to reduce stress as well as promoting restful sleep.

5. Plan breaks in your day

The aim here is to allow time for the unexpected (which, as we all know, will happen!). Get up 15 minutes earlier than you think you need to and prepare for the day without rushing. Even better, get things ready the night before. Try to have 20 minutes in the morning and afternoon that is exclusively 'your' time, in which you can do whatever you want, even if it is simply sitting doing nothing. Look forward to these times when things get busy and if you are unable to use them always remember to 'catch up' later on.

And one thing not to do . . .

One approach, on the other hand, to avoid, is that of using smoking and alcohol as crutches to help you cope – in the long run they simply make stress worse. Drinking more to 'calm your nerves' is a slippery slope.

■ Dr Henderson is a GP and medical columnist who is a regular contributor to *The Sunday Times* and other national papers and magazines. His book, *Stress Beaters – 100 Proven Ways to Manage Stress*, is published by Metro Books at £7.99.

. . . and five more simple stress relievers

Ingrid Miller offers five handy stressbusting techniques to use in everyday situations . . .

1. Stretch

Sitting upright on a chair, and keeping your back straight, extend your arms out in front of you as far as possible. Hold for ten seconds. Repeat, with your arms behind you. Then hold on to the sides of your chair and push your body upwards. Feel your spine stretch. Hold for ten. Now stretch arms to the ceiling, to release tension in back and shoulders. Relax and shake your arms.

2. Use scent to improve your mood

Certain aromas are thought to activate the production of the brain's feel-good chemical serotonin [although one recent research study suggests that the benefits claimed for aromatherapy may derive from the power of suggestion. Ed.]. Drip a few drops of the following aromatherapy

> *Try to have 20 minutes in the morning and afternoon that is exclusively 'your' time, in which you can do whatever you want*

oils on a tissue to sniff when you feel stress levels rising: jasmine, neroli, lavender, chamomile, vetiver, clary sage.

3. De-clutter

Mess creates confusion and a sense of loss of power. If your desk/home/car is messy and disorganised, have a good clear out and tidy up. You'll instantly feel more in control.

4. Change the habit

Many stresses are habitual. If you start to feel anxious or stressed out, do something out of character. Stop what you're doing and do something else. Or take a minute to take stock and work out why you're feeling uptight.

5. Think positive

Use 'affirmations' – positive strands of thought put into words. Repeating, 'I am a loving and much loved person', can work wonders. Say it and believe it. And it will become true.

■ Ingrid Millar is the agony aunt of *Essentials* Magazine.

■ The above information is from www.stressbusting.co.uk

© Dr Roger Henderson and Ingrid Millar

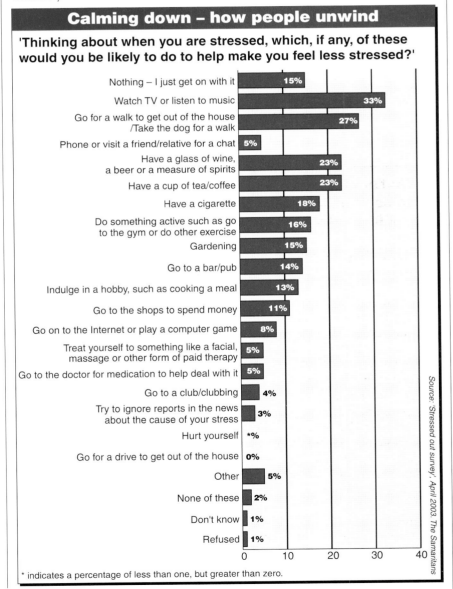

Calming down – how people unwind

'Thinking about when you are stressed, which, if any, of these would you be likely to do to help make you feel less stressed?'

	%
Nothing – I just get on with it	15%
Watch TV or listen to music	33%
Go for a walk to get out of the house /Take the dog for a walk	27%
Phone or visit a friend/relative for a chat	5%
Have a glass of wine, a beer or a measure of spirits	23%
Have a cup of tea/coffee	23%
Have a cigarette	18%
Do something active such as go to the gym or do other exercise	16%
Gardening	15%
Go to a bar/pub	14%
Indulge in a hobby, such as cooking a meal	13%
Go to the shops to spend money	11%
Go on to the Internet or play a computer game	8%
Treat yourself to something like a facial, massage or other form of paid therapy	5%
Go to the doctor for medication to help deal with it	5%
Go to a club/clubbing	4%
Try to ignore reports in the news about the cause of your stress	3%
Hurt yourself	*%
Go for a drive to get out of the house	0%
Other	5%
None of these	2%
Don't know	1%
Refused	1%

* indicates a percentage of less than one, but greater than zero.

Source: 'Stressed out survey', April 2003. The Samaritans

You feel what you eat

Stress can contribute to a long list of health problems, says Suzannah Olivier, but there are ways to boost your resistance, including eating the right sort of food

Chronic stress is a contributory factor to many illnesses. It can lead to low energy, skin complaints such as eczema and spots, poor wound healing, increased susceptibility to colds and flu, tension headaches, fuzzy thinking, loss of libido, raised blood pressure, and much more.

But with a sensible approach to diet there are ways of reducing the effects of stress and helping your body to remain healthy.

How stress contributes to health problems

The stress response triggers off high levels of the hormones adrenalin and cortisol. These are produced regardless of the type of stress experienced, from emergencies (an impending car accident, for example) to slower-acting stresses (such as pressure at work, traffic jams or drinking coffee).

These stress hormones use up significant amounts of vitamin C, B-vitamins, magnesium and zinc, because it's an emergency, they take priority over the body's general use for these nutrients. This means that, for example, vitamin C and zinc are not sufficiently available for collagen production to keep skin clear and to make white blood cells to fend off infections; B-vitamins are not fully available for energy production and mental function; while depleted magnesium will increase the likelihood of headaches and raised blood pressure.

With a sensible approach to diet there are ways of reducing the effects of stress and helping your body to remain healthy

---

Increased stress levels also raise the amount of oxidation damage, which affects various body tissues, and constantly raised cortisol levels keep the body in a 'catabolic' state which interferes with tissue repair.

Increase your resistance to the effects of stress

We can't always avoid stress in our lives, but by eating foods that ensure we provide the nutrients needed both for the stress reaction and for healthy tissue building, we can reduce the negative effects of stress on the body.

You can think of it as building a nutritional shield to protect you against the slings and arrows that stress throws at you.

Foods rich in stress-busting nutrients

A balanced diet – one that supplies stress hormones, provides anti-oxidants to fend off oxidation damage, and keeps brain chemicals, such as serotonin, steady for improved moods – should feature:

- At least five portions of fruit and vegetables daily, preferably 7-8 portions. A portion is 80g/3oz, so for instance: one apple, 2 plums, 3 dried apricots, 1/2 cup chopped vegetables, 1/2 cup beans or pulses, one wine-glassful of fruit or vegetable juice.
- Lean meats such as fish, skinless chicken or turkey meat, game or red meat with all the fat cut off, or vegetarian protein sources such as low-fat dairy produce, pulses, soya-based foods, Quorn, nuts and seeds.
- Whole grains such as wholemeal bread, brown rice, wholewheat pasta, rye, porridge oats and jacket potatoes, or unusual grains such as quinoa, buckwheat or wholewheat couscous.

- Healthy fats from virgin olive oil, cold pressed walnut, sesame, sunflower or safflower oils, unsalted nuts and seeds, avocado.

The stressbusting nutrients themselves can be found in the following foods:

Zinc
Lean meat, seafood (especially oysters), whole wheat, popcorn, muesli, eggs, yoghurt, cheese, nuts, seeds

Vitamin C
All fruit and vegetables, especially citrus fruit, strawberries, black-berries, kiwi, cabbage and broccoli

B-vitamins
All wholegrains, yeast extract, yoghurt, liver, dates, molasses, pumpkin, beans, avocado

Magnesium
Dark green leafy vegetables, grape-fruit, figs, sweet-corn, seeds and nuts, aubergines, raisins, carrots, tomatoes

Foods to avoid
In addition to psychological and physical stresses, there are also nutritional stresses. Each time you drink alcohol or a cup of coffee, for instance, it impacts on your body's ability to handle stress. This does not mean that you need to abstain all the time, just be aware of the effects they can have and minimise your consumption of them at stressful times in your life.

Each time you drink alcohol or a cup of coffee, for instance, it impacts on your body's ability to handle stress

---

Sugar is devoid of vitamins and minerals and also uses up nutrients such as B-vitamins. Replace with a little raw honey, puréed sweet fruit, dates.

Caffeine raises stress hormones and can lead to insomnia. Caffeine is found in coffee, tea, colas, the herb guarana, pain medication. Replace with caffeine-free coffee or tea, sparkling water with juice, fruit and herb teas, barley coffee.

Alcohol is a depressant and is dehydrating. Stick to a maximum of 7 units weekly if a woman and 14 units weekly if a man. Match each alcoholic drink with a large glass of water.

Cigarettes use up antioxidants. Give up smoking or at least eat extra fruit and vegetables.

Nature's little helpers
Ideally, you should be able to get all you need from a well-balanced diet. However, you may want to add an antioxidant formula supplement to your regime at times of stress. There are also some herbal supplements that can help to counteract stress:

Liquorice Root balances stress hormones. Some formulae include ginseng, another 'adaptogen' which helps the body to adapt to stress (do not use liquorice root if you have high blood pressure). Kava Kava has an anxiety reducing, calming effect and is good for migraines. Nicknamed the herbal valium, St John's Wort is effective in trials for moderate depression. Works by improving serotonin levels in the brain.

Please note
If you are pregnant, breast-feeding or taking prescribed medication for any condition then herbal and nutritional supplements must only be taken with professional advice. If these restrictions do not apply, then take the dose suggested on the bottle.

- Suzannah Olivier is a health writer and author of several nutrition books including *The Stress Protection Plan*, *Maximising Energy* and *500 of the most important stress-busting tips you'll ever need*. Visit her website at www.healthandnutrition.co.uk

- The above information is from www. stressbusting.co.uk
© Suzannah Olivier

Right sort of stress can be good for health

By Kate Howard

A brief bout of stress can be good for you, according to new research. The primeval fight or flight response can strengthen the immune system but long-term, or chronic, stress weakens the body's defences, the study by researchers in the United States and Canada shows.

Chronic stress is caused by events that turn a person's world upside down, for example becoming permanently disabled, caring for a spouse with dementia or becoming a refugee.

But acute or short-term stress caused by events which have a resolution or end point such as exams or public speaking was found to boost the immune system.

The evidence presented by Dr Suzanne Segerstrom and Dr Gregory Miller in the American Psychological Association journal *Psychological Bulletin* shows that short-term stress 'revs up' the immune system to prepare the body for injury or infection, but long-term stress wears it down.

The findings come as separate research found increasing numbers of British workers were taking time off due to stress.

A survey of 1,100 employers by the Chartered Institute of Personnel and Development showed that workers took an average of 9.12 days off ill last year, with larger numbers than before blaming heavy workloads and pressure to meet targets for their ill-health.

© *Telegraph Group Limited, London 2005*

KEY FACTS

■ Everyone feels stressed at times. You may feel under pressure, worried, tense, upset, sad, angry – or maybe a mixture of uncomfortable feelings. (p. 1)

■ Although many people will experience stress and anxiety to varying degrees, between 5% to 10% of young people will have anxiety problems that are bad enough to affect their ability to live a normal life. (p. 2)

■ Many people think exam stress is a teenage problem, but it can happen to people of all ages. (p. 3)

■ During the last year (1 April 2003 to 31 March 2004) more than 900 children and young people called ChildLine's free, 24-hour helpline about the stress caused by their exams – up from just over 600 during the previous twelve months. (p. 4)

■ Stressed-out people have higher blood pressure, and where stress-levels hit boiling point sufferers are at a higher risk of death from any cause than their more chilled-out colleagues. (p. 5)

■ Give yourself time to relax and get over the exams. Forget about them for as long as you can. Waiting for the results to arrive can also be a stressful time. (p. 6)

■ Most of us would like to think that childhood is a time of happiness and innocence. The reality is that children are under just as much pressure as the rest of us. (p. 8)

■ Anxiety over heavy workloads, long hours and the threat of redundancy is fuelling an epidemic of stress, with 58 per cent of union health and safety representatives citing it as the major cause of complaints – outstripping conditions such as back pain and repetitive strain injury. (p. 11)

■ The three professions that scored worst for physical ill health related to work stress were ambulance service employees, teachers and social workers. (p. 12)

■ Young people are the most stressed out on a daily basis, with 24% of those aged 15-24 getting wound up every day. (p. 13)

■ Women were slightly more likely to say that their stress levels have increased in the past five years compared to men – 42% of women compared to 38% of men. (p. 13)

■ The UK Department of Health state that 3.6% of national average salary budget is paid to employees off sick with stress. Stress is now officially the Number One cause of sickness absence although 20% of employers still do not regard stress as a health and safety issue. (p. 14)

■ UK plc needs to sit up and take notice, because the cost to industry is huge. Over 91 million working days are lost each year due to mental ill health, at an estimated cost to industry of £4 billion. (p. 17)

■ The survey of more than 2,000 people found that frequent worrying was twice as common in women as men – 16% compared to 8%. (p. 19)

■ Each new case of work-related stress leads to an average of 29 days off work. The Health and Safety Executive estimates that 13.4 million working days were lost to stress and anxiety in 2001. (p. 20)

■ Anxiety is an unpleasant feeling of fear and apprehension. Normally anxiety can be useful, helping us to avoid dangerous situations, making us alert and giving us the motivation to deal with problems. (p. 21)

■ More than 700,000 people – a quarter of all claims – receive up to £84 a week in incapacity benefit on the grounds of poor mental health, a 38 per cent increase since 1997. Of those, 232,300 are women, a 60 per cent increase in seven years. (p. 23)

■ Stress and anxiety both require energy, and once this energy is used up, the person becomes depressed; there is no energy left to feed the anxieties, so they are never resolved. (p. 24)

■ Under stress, people become demotivated and forgetful, and are less able to concentrate. (p. 25)

■ An estimated 13.5 million days are lost each year due to self-reported work-related stress, depression or anxiety, costing the economy £7bn a year in sick pay, lost productivity and health costs. (p. 26)

■ Try to make time to switch off from your tasks at home or at work. Use your free time to relax and unwind. (p. 29)

■ Physical activity is an important means of reducing stress levels and preventing some of its damaging effects on the body. (p. 30)

■ Changing your lifestyle in this way can make you feel physically fitter and better able to cope with some of the demands on you – and more able to cope with stressful situations. (p. 31)

■ Research has shown that around 12 million adults see their GPs with mental health problems each year. Most of these suffer from anxiety and depression, much of it stress related. (p. 33)

■ With a sensible approach to diet there are ways of reducing the effects of stress and helping your body to remain healthy. (p. 38)

ADDITIONAL RESOURCES

You might like to contact the following organisations for further information. Due to the increasing cost of postage, many organisations cannot respond to enquiries unless they receive a stamped, addressed envelope.

British Heart Foundation (BHF)
14 Fitzhardinge Street
London, W1H 4DH
Tel: 020 7935 0185
Fax: 020 7486 5820
E-mail: internet@bhf.org.uk
Website: www.bhf.org.uk
Plays a leading role in the fight against heart disease and death by ways including educating the public and health professionals about heart disease, its prevention and treatment.

Chartered Institute of Personnel and Development (CIPD)
151 The Broadway
Wimbledon
London, SW19 1JQ
Tel: 020 8971 9000
Fax: 020 8263 3333
E-mail: ipd@cipd.co.uk
Website: www.cipd.co.uk
www.peoplemanagement.co.uk
The professional body for those involved in the management and development of people.

Chartered Management Institute
Professional Manager
2 Savoy Court
Strand, London, WC2R 0EZ
Tel: 020 7497 0580
Fax: 020 7497 0463
E-mail:
publications@managers.org.uk
Website: www.managers.org.uk
The Chartered Management Institute shapes and supports the managers of tomorrow.

ChildLine
45 Folgate Street
London, E1 6GL
Tel: 020 7650 3200
Fax: 020 7650 3201
E-mail: reception@childline.org.uk
Website: www.childline.org.uk
Children can call ChildLine on 0800 1111 (all calls are free of charge, 24 hours a day, 365 days a year).

International Stress Management Association (UK)
PO Box 348
Waltham Cross, EN8 8ZL
Tel: 07000 780430
Fax: 01992 426673
E-mail: stress@isma.org.uk
Website: www.isma.org.uk
ISMA (UK) exists to promote sound knowledge and best practice in the prevention and reduction of human stress.

Mental Health Foundation
Sea Containers House
20 Upper Ground
London, SE1 9QB
Tel: 020 7803 1100
Fax: 020 7803 1111
E-mail: mhf@mhf.org.uk
Website: www.mentalhealth.org.uk
The Mental Health Foundation is the leading UK charity working in mental health and learning disabilities.

MIND
Granta House, 15-19 Broadway
Stratford
London, E15 4BQ
Tel: 020 8519 2122
Fax: 020 8522 1725
E-mail: contact@mind.org.uk
Website: www.mind.org.uk
Mind works for a better life for everyone with experience of mental distress. For a full publications list send a stamped addressed envelope to Mind Mail Order, 15-19 Broadway, London E15 4BQ.

The National Youth Agency (NYA)
19-23 Humberstone Road
Leicester, LE5 3GJ
Tel: 0116 242 7350
Fax: 0116 242 7471
E-mail: nya@nya.org.uk
Website: www.nya.org.uk
www.youthinformation.com
Aims to advance youth work to promote young people's personal and social development, and their voice, influence and place in society.

Royal College of Psychiatrists
17 Belgrave Square
London, SW1X 8PG
Tel: 020 7235 2351
Fax: 020 7235 1935
E-mail: rcpsych@rcpsych.ac.uk
Website: www.rcpsych.ac.uk
Produces an excellent series of free leaflets on various aspects of mental health. Supplied free of charge but a stamped, addressed envelope is required.

The Samaritans
The Upper Mill
Kingston Road
Ewell, Surrey, KT17 2AF
Tel: 020 8394 8300
Fax: 020 8394 8301
E-mail: jo@samaritans.org.uk
Website: www.samaritans.org.uk
Deals with suicide-related issues. Their help line is open 24 hours a day 08457 90 90 90.

Stress Management Society
PO Box 193
Harrow, HA1 3ZE
Tel: 0870 199 3260
E-mail: info@stress.org.uk
Website: www.stress.org.uk
The on-line community that's taking people from distress to de-stress.

Success Unlimited
PO Box 67
Didcot, OX11 9YS
Website:
www.successunlimited.co.uk
www.bullyonline.org
Helpline Tel. 01235 212286
answerphone.

UK National Work-Stress Network
9 Bell Lane
Syresham
Brackley, NN13 5HP
Tel: 07966 196033
Fax: 01280 850056
Website: www.workstress.net
Campaigns for European and UK Legislation on Work Stress.

INDEX

National Youth Agency (NYA), and exam stress 6
nurses, and young people and stress 2
nutritional supplements, and stress relief 39

older people, and stress 13

panic attacks
    and exam stress 7
    and young people 2
parents
    and stress 13
    and stress in young people 1, 2
        exam stress 5
phobias, and young people 2
physical abuse, and stress 1, 2
positive thinking, and stress relief 37
priests, and young people and stress 2
psychologists, and young people and stress 2
psychotherapists, and young people and stress 2
public sector workers, and workplace stress 11

relaxation, coping with stress 29-30, 31-2, 34, 36-7
Royal College of Psychiatrists, *Mental Health and Growing Up* 1-2

Samaritans
    and statistics on stress 13
    and stress in young people 2
schools
    young people and stress 1
        exam stress 3-6
        and meditation 9-10
self-hypnosis, and stress 27
sexual abuse, and stress 1, 2
sickness absence, and workplace stress 15
sleep
    and stress 19, 27, 29
        exam stress 3, 6, 7
smoking, and stress 19, 27, 31, 34, 35, 37
social workers
    and stress in young people 2
    and workplace stress 12
stress
    and anxiety 2, 21
    coping with 27-39
        case studies 31, 32
        exercise 19, 27, 30, 34, 36, 37
        and healthy eating 30, 31, 34, 35, 38-9
        increasing resistance to effects of 38
        keeping a diary 36
        planning breaks in the day 37
        positive action 29
        positive thinking 37
        protecting your heart 31-2
        relaxation 29-30, 31-2, 34, 36-7
        seeking help and support 32, 34
        self-help 34
        the stress chain 32
        stress management 32, 36
        and time management 27, 29, 32, 36
    defining 1, 5, 33
    factors determining degree of 14-15
    'fight or flight' response to 1, 14-15, 25, 28

harmful effects of 28, 38
health benefits of the right sort of 39
and lifestyle 19, 31-2
National Stress Awareness Day 26
positive and negative 14
regional variations in experiences of 13
signs and symptoms of 1, 2, 5, 12, 28-9, 33, 35
statistics on 13, 19
see also workplace stress; young people and stress
stress management 32, 36
stretching exercises, and stress relief 37
support groups, and stress 32

teachers
    and stress in young people 1
        exam stress 6
    and workplace stress 12
technological change, and workplace stress 16
time management, and stress 27, 29, 32, 36
trade unions, and workplace stress 11, 26
training, and workplace stress 16
transcendental meditation 9-10

unemployment, and incapacity benefit 23
university admissions, and exam stress 7

women
    and stress 13
        frequent worrying 19
workplace stress 11-26
    and bullying 14-15
    and the 'can't cope culture' 23
    causes of 15-16
    and changes in working practices 11, 26
    and communication 15
    coping with 24
    costs of 14, 23
    health risks of 20
    and health and safety 14
    and incapacity benefit 23
    and the law 17, 20, 22
    and managers 18, 25
    and mental health 17-18
    and public sector workers 11
    stopping stressing about 26
    triggers 12
    TUC survey of 11

yoga, and exam stress 5
young people and stress 1-10
    and anxiety 2
    causes of stress 1, 2
    children 8-10
    coping with stress 1
    effects of stress 1, 2
    exam stress 3-7, 9
    and frequent worrying 19
    getting help 1-2
    and meditation 5, 8-10
    statistics 13

Zen Buddhism, and Kinhin (walking meditation) 10

ACKNOWLEDGEMENTS

The publisher is grateful for permission to reproduce the following material.

While every care has been taken to trace and acknowledge copyright, the publisher tenders its apology for any accidental infringement or where copyright has proved untraceable. The publisher would be pleased to come to a suitable arrangement in any such case with the rightful owner.

Chapter One: Young People and Stress

Coping with stress, © Royal College of Psychiatrists, Anxiety and stress, © Lewisham Child and Adolescent Mental Health Services 2004, Exam stress, © Crown copyright is reproduced with the permission of Her Majesty's Stationery Office, Major rise in exam stress calls to ChildLine, © ChildLine, Exam stress, © ChildLine, Exam result stress, © TheSite.org, Dealing with exam stress, © National Youth Agency (NYA), Stressed students seek medical help, © Guardian Newspapers Limited 2004, The student experience, © UNITE/MORI, Meditation for children, © www.ivillage.co.uk.

Chapter Two: Stress in the Workplace

Stress and the workforce, © Guardian Newspapers Limited 2004, Stress levels at work, © Trades Union Congress, Stressful careers, © Telegraph Group Limited, London 2005, Stressed out, © The Samaritans, Stress levels, © The Samaritans, Stress and bullying, © Success Unlimited, Common causes of stress, © NHS Health Scotland, Health and Safety Authority Ireland, Health and Safety Executive GB, Suffering in silence, © Chartered Management Institute, Stress keeps four in ten awake at night, © 2005 Associated Newspapers Ltd, Stressed out, © PruHealth Report, Anxiety attack, © Chartered Institute of Personnel and Development, Anxiety and stress, © TheSite.org, The emotional effects of stress, © The Samaritans, The law and stress, © UK National Work-Stress Network 2005, 'Can't cope culture' bill hits £2bn and rising, © Telegraph Group Limited, London 2005, Incapacity benefits, © Crown copyright is reproduced with the permission of Her Majesty's Stationery Office, Cope with stress at work, © The Stress Management Society, Managing stress in others, © Chartered Management Institute, Let's stop stressing about stress, © Guardian Newspapers Limited 2004.

Chapter Three: Coping with Stress

A ten-step guide to coping with stress, © The Stress Management Society, Managing stress, © 2004 Mind, Stress and your heart, © British Heart Foundation, The stress chain, © British Heart Foundation, Stress and how to cope with it, © Mental Health Foundation, 'Life should be fun!', © International Stress Management Association (UK), Top 10 tips for busting stress, © Dr Roger Henderson and Ingrid Millar, Calming down – how people unwind, © The Samaritans, You feel what you eat, © Suzannah Olivier, Right sort of stress can be good for you, © Telegraph Group Limited, London 2005.

Photographs and illustrations:

Pages 1, 10, 24, 30, 38: Simon Kneebone; pages 3, 16, 35: Don Hatcher; pages 5, 22: Pumpkin House; pages 8, 27: Bev Aisbett; pages 14, 33: Angelo Madrid.

Craig Donnellan
Cambridge
April, 2005

First published by Independence
PO Box 295
Cambridge CB1 3XP
England

British Library Cataloguing in Publication Data
Stress and Anxiety – (Issues Series)
I. Donnellan, Craig II. Series
155.9'042

ISBN 1 86168 314 6

Printed in Great Britain
MWL Print Group Ltd

Typeset by
Claire Boyd

Cover
The illustration on the front cover is by
Pumpkin House.

Stress and Anxiety

Independence

Educational Publishers
Cambridge